CYNTHIA HICKEY

EXPOSURE AT SEA

Cynthia Hickey

ISBN-13: 978-1-0881-6947-6

When you lie down among the sheep,
you are like the wings of a dove covered with silver,
and the end of its wings with shining gold.

-Psalm 68:13

1

woman screamed.

Molly Nicholson jerked, spun, and almost
knocked her camera off its tripod.
A man held a woman around the waist, and swung her
with a sheer look of joy on her face as she leaned back.
His laugh rang over the milling crowd of passengers.
Molly smiled at their matching tee shirts. Must be
newlyweds.

She relaxed and turned to survey the ship docked in
front of her. Her new job as a photographer aboard
Midnight Cruise Lines couldn't have come at a better
time. She needed some fun in her life.

An ocean breeze teased her hair, and she lifted her
face to greet it, filling her lungs with the fresh, moist air
of Honolulu. Closing her eyes, she breathed a prayer of
thanksgiving. The sun caressed her cheeks, and Molly
smiled. She'd be sailing in a couple of hours on her
dream job.

"You must be Molly."

She opened her eyes to a curvy woman with a
bouncy ponytail the color of mahogany. The woman
thrust out her hand in welcome. "I'm Suzy Harkin, the
events coordinator. I'm so pleased to meet you. We'll
be great friends. I just know it. Aren't you excited? I

always am when embarking on a new adventure."

Molly's smile widened at Suzy's exuberance. "Where would you like me to stand?"

"Right here by this sign. When the passengers are ready to board, they'll pause long enough for you to snap their picture." Suzy handed Molly several sheets of paper. "Here are some of the events we'd like you to attend. Your main job is to offer our passengers photos of their fun times. You'll switch off with Daniella, our other photographer. That way, you'll have lots of time to enjoy yourself. See you later!" With a wave of her fingers, Suzy bounded up the gangplank.

The happy couple continued to cavort like children, and Molly snapped their photo as the groom swept his bride into his arms in a traditional across-the-threshold lift. The woman giggled and buried her face in his neck. Molly sighed. The sight of them wrapped up in their love withered Molly's heart. Would she ever know such joy in the arms of a man? Not likely. With her penchant for choosing some real winners, the task seemed monumental.

Over the next couple of hours, she took photo after photo of smiling, laughing, tourists until she thought her face would freeze in a perpetual grin and her finger fall off from clicking the shutter button. She ought to be more grateful. How often did a girl get to accept a job on one of the most luxurious cruise lines in North America?

Another passenger hurried toward the gangplank. Molly lifted her camera. "Smile."

"No pictures." The man flung up a hand to block the lens, and rushed past. Details of his profile registered in Molly's mind. Salt and pepper hair. Black polo shirt. Khaki pants. Footsteps pounding as he dashed onboard.

"Have a wonderful trip anyway." Molly lowered her arms. How rude.

Leaning against the iron railing, she surveyed the surroundings. Across a narrow asphalt drive, sat an ugly nondescript warehouse. Grey brick. Tall windows, some broken. The faint odor of fuel mixed with the aroma of exotic flowers. The passenger photos would be nicer without such an unattractive backdrop. Considering the expense of sailing Midnight Cruise Lines, you'd think they'd dock somewhere more upscale. She searched for a better place to stand.

"You can take mine, if you'd like." A voice rumbled across her as gentle as a summer rain.

"Smile." She raised the camera to focus and froze. His inky hair ruffled in the ocean breeze. Any man who appeared this good through the camera lens must look incredible on the other side of the camera.

Eyes as dark as Mississippi mud sparkled, and a dimple winked from his right cheek. He hooked his thumb through his belt loop and leaned against a post. Uh-oh. Devastatingly handsome, and he knew it.

The sling on his arm didn't detract from his appearance. Instead, Molly wanted to help him. She'd always been one to pick up wounded strays. Not anymore. This was one clipped bird she'd stay far away from. She clicked the button a few times. The man's good looks begged to be frozen in time.

"All done. You can purchase photos any evening after five o'clock in the gift shop." Molly pasted on her "professional" smile.

"Will you be selling them?" The man towered over

her five-foot-two frame. His gaze flicked to her name tag.

"No, I, uh, will be working." Molly straightened to appear taller and tried to focus her attention on her equipment. Anywhere but on the handsome stranger.

"Okay, Molly. I'll see you around. My name's Lance. It's nice to meet you." He gave her a mock salute and strolled onto the ship.

Gracious. She put a hand to her chest to slow her heart rate and stared after him until another passenger claimed her attention.

*

Lance Spencer had almost turned tail and run when he'd seen the sprite behind the camera. Except those sea-blue eyes and corn silk curls reeled him in like one of those deep sea bass he hoped to. After meeting her, taking the cruise while healing seemed like an even better idea. Why not indulge in a harmless flirtation at sea? Fun for a week, then walk away. Wasn't that what his buddies advised?

With another glance over his shoulder, he proceeded up the gangplank. People milled about the deck. Another woman, identified as Suzy by the name tag, helped direct lost passengers. A man in a white medical jacket answered the questions of an elderly couple. By the way he kept glancing at the clock, Lance knew he had somewhere else to be. Lance smiled and moved inside.

An older man, wearing an expensive polo shirt and khaki pants, slumped on a sofa, while a red-faced bellboy apologized profusely for losing his bags. A vase of orchids filled the air with perfume.

A city on the waves. He'd feel right at home. Now,

as long as he reminded himself he was on a much-needed vacation, he'd be fine. He glanced at the ticket in his laptop bag. Cabin 3106. Plaza deck. An ocean-view stateroom.

He quickened his step and shot out a hand. "Hold the elevator!"

Crowded shoulder-to-shoulder, passengers stood in a silent clump and avoided each other's eyes. Lance smiled. No time to make new friends, obviously. The irate man with the lost luggage squeezed inside and pressed the button for the Penthouse level.

Lance raised his eyebrows. He'd thought about a cabin on the Penthouse deck, but holding onto most of his savings seemed the wiser choice. He didn't plan to spend a lot of time in his room.

Exiting on his floor, he found his cabin, first door on his right, and inserted his key. Across the small space an azure sky filled the window. Two over-sized twin beds occupied the wall opposite. A closet of a bathroom, a small table with two chairs, a television, and this was home for the next week. His luggage lay on top of one of the beds. His garment bag hung from a hook on the back of the door. A brochure with meal and show times lay on the table next to an itinerary and another vase of sweet-smelling flowers. He chuckled. There'd be glimpses of the tropics around every corner it seemed.

Two hours until dinner. Plenty of time for a short nap. Lance flopped across the empty bed and closed his eyes. There was no one he needed to wave goodbye to. Let the other passengers toss confetti. The ship rocked as it pulled away from the dock, a whistle blew, and images of a curly-haired photographer with a dusting of freckles flickered across his mind.

*

Molly dropped the camera's SIM card at the photo lab and shuffled to the miniscule cabin she shared with one of the waitresses. With dinner in thirty minutes, Hilga wasn't in.

With a sigh, Molly kicked off her shoes. The cruise lines insisted the employees dress nice in the evenings, and Molly's favorite little black dress hung in the closet. Too bad the look wouldn't have the same va-va-va-voom with practical flats on her feet. Comfort above all else, right?

She headed for the closet-like bathroom; big enough for a stand-up shower, pedestal sink, and a toilet. Turning the water to hot, she shed her clothes and stepped in. Minutes later, shower complete, Molly dressed in a cotton robe, grabbed her Bible, and pounced on the bed. She turned to Psalms and let the words soothe away the stress of the day.

"Better wake up." Hilga's words ricocheted around the cabin. Molly's eyes flew open as her roommate ducked out of the room. "Bob's having a coronary."

The bedside clock glowed with 6:15. "Oh, no." Dinner call was fifteen minutes ago. Molly scrambled from the bed and snatched her dress from the hanger. Thank God she'd put her makeup on before reading. Her hair didn't require maintenance. There wasn't anything she could do to tame it anyway. She grabbed her badge and camera, then dashed after Hilga.

A stream of laughing passengers made their way to the restaurant. Molly kept a grin she hoped didn't resemble a grimace on her face, and speed walked past them to enter the restaurant ahead of the large group.

She burst into the spacious dining area and came face-to-face with the chief purser's frown. Bob pointed at his watch. Molly mouthed, "I'm sorry" and mingled to snap photos of couples enjoying their first meal onboard.

The tantalizing aromas of beef and exotic foods filled the air. Molly's stomach growled, reminding her she'd worked through lunch.

When Lance strolled in, her heart almost stopped, and she switched directions in order to concentrate on her job. It ought to be a sin to look as yummy as he did.

"Molly." Antonio, a small, wiry man that developed the cruise's photos hissed her name from around the corner to the kitchen.

"You have the pictures ready?"

"Ready for purchase. Except one." He glanced from side to side. "I need you to look at something. Can you come to the lab?"

"In about thirty minutes."

Antonio frowned. "This is important."

Molly glanced in Bob's direction. He chatted with a table full of passengers.

Please, God, don't let me get fired my first night.

"Okay, but we have to be quick."

"This will be worth it. Trust me." He sprinted toward the stairs.

Molly followed. Her short legs prevented her from keeping Antonio's pace. By the time they reached the lab, blisters formed on her heels. Once safely inside, Antonio locked the door behind them, grabbed her arm, and dragged her to the table in the center of the lab. Molly glanced his way then down.

"What?" The photo was the one she'd snapped of

the honeymoon couple in front of the warehouse.

"Look close. In the window behind them."

Molly gasped. Two definite silhouettes. One with its hands wrapped around the throat of the other.

"We need to find out who they are." Molly lifted the picture by the corner.

"Won't be hard. They're passengers."

"You know them?"

Antonio shrugged. "I was … sneaking a smoke around the corner. I heard shouts and peeked. Two men. One middle-aged with salt and pepper hair and wearing a polo shirt. The other, younger, not as well dressed. Maybe staff here on ship."

"You didn't see their faces?"

"Not good. I might recognize the passenger. I saw his profile. The other had his back to me."

"Should we tell the captain?"

Antonio shook his head. "Not yet. Let me make another copy of the photo. I'll get it to you when I've finished printing the rest of the pictures."

"Okay." She could check to see whether anyone missed reporting for work once the ship sailed. The other man with the graying hair would be more difficult to locate. Half the passenger list probably contained men with the color hair Antonio described.

"You need to be careful." Antonio tried to grab the photo. Molly held it behind her back.

"Why?"

"The taller one looked your way when the camera flash went off."

2

Lance spotted the pretty photographer the moment she scooted back into the restaurant. Face pale, hair wilder than usual. A secret rendezvous? He grinned. She didn't seem the type. But experience taught him gorgeous women often held ugly secrets. Little Miss Molly would provide entertainment on the cruise, nothing more. He turned his attention to the man sitting next to him and half-listened as he tried to sell him a time-share in Florida.

Across from him sat the previously flustered fellow who'd been missing his luggage. Considering the linen shirt and black pants he wore, he'd either bought new clothes, or found the ones he'd lost. The man's eyes flitted from one table to another as he pushed his food around his plate. Maybe he waited for someone. He'd introduced himself as Robert Morrison, CEO of an import/export business. Said he was on the cruise for business reasons. Could there be a partner somewhere?

Lance shrugged. What did he really do? Seemed like if someone didn't want to tell you what they really did, they said import/export, and Lance had yet to see the man with anyone.

Pity for the man to waste the dinner. Lance forked another bite of salmon. Coated with a crunchy sweet topping, the meat practically melted in his mouth. The food was among the best he'd ever eaten. And Molly could be a pleasant decoration. Or did he mean diversion? Becoming an idle playboy was foreign. He waved her over.

She seemed to glide. The overhead lights cast a golden glow around her curls. All the woman lacked was wings and she'd be the perfect portrait of an angel.

"Photos anyone?" Her wide eyes paused on each person at the table, lingering a moment on the two middle-aged men.

Was she searching for someone in particular? Lance set down his fork. "We have an empty seat. Can you join us?"

"No, but thank you. I'm on until eight." She lifted her Nikon D700. "A group shot?"

"Maybe I'll see you around." Lance lifted a glass of sparkling water in her direction.

With one more glance around the table, Molly stepped back. Her foot caught a chair leg and she grabbed Mr. Morrison's shoulder to break her fall. He slapped her hand away, then leaped from his seat. "Get off me!"

Molly's eyes widened in fear. "I'm sorry."

Lance's face heated and he stood, prepared to defend the frightened woman. "Mr. Morrison, she meant no harm."

His jaw clenched. "My apologies. I'm feeling seasick. Excuse me." With one more scathing glance at her, he stormed away.

Molly's chin quivered. "I really was sorry."

Lance moved to her side. "No harm done." The others murmured their agreement. He pulled out a chair and lowered her into it. "Sit for a moment. I'll clear it with the purser if I need to."

"No, really, I'm fine. Just embarrassed." She pushed to her feet. "I have a job to do. Thank you, gentlemen." Her cheeks reddened. Squaring her shoulders, she gave them a nod, and marched out of sight.

She'd seemed troubled. Almost frightened. He decided to find her after dinner and see whether she needed his help.

After he finished eating, Lance strolled the ship. He found Molly leaning on the railing, staring out at the inky water. The moon lit the tips of her curls with silver. The evening's salty breeze teased at her hair and the hem of her skirt. He'd never seen a lovelier vision. The vulnerable expression on her face tugged at his heart. For the first time since stepping onboard, he questioned his plan of using her for a fling.

She wasn't like the other women he'd dated. Molly exuded innocence with the girl next door charm. No, he wouldn't toy with her affections. He'd settle for friendship. Someone to pass the time with while onboard.

Without speaking, he moved in beside her and gazed over the wide expanse of the ocean, marveling at God's creation. Waves lapped against the boat. He raised his head to watch the lone seagull soar overhead.

He'd visited the vastness of Montana, the mountains of Alabama, and now gazed over an endless ocean. It'd been a long time since he'd contemplated on anything God did. Work took up too much of his time. He needed this break. Hopefully, the cruise would heal more than a bullet hole in his shoulder.

Molly jerked. "Are you following me?" She turned to face him.

Did that frighten her? "Are you running?"

She gave a delicate shrug. "Depends. The ship is full of women who have the time to spend with you. Why does it seem that you're focused on me?"

"I don't know." She was right. Something about her drew him to her. Maybe it was her impish ways. A light-hearted woman like Molly would feel like a vacation after Abigail and her moods. Who was he kidding? Life as a detective didn't leave time for romance.

"It seems like something's bothering you," Lance said when she turned back to the sea. "Can I help?"

"Not unless you're a cop." The words slipped out as if they'd been coated with butter. Molly clapped a hand over her mouth.

"This might be your lucky day." Lance motioned toward a nearby bench. "Let's sit."

*

Molly shook her head. "No, I'm just running off at the mouth. See you in the morning." She practically ran back to her cabin. Idiot. What was she thinking? If the man in the photo knew she'd told anyone, she'd be next. Killers were all the same. She read books. She watched movies. There was a target on her back as big as the ship.

She paused, remembering the man who'd raced past her before the ship left the dock. He'd had salt-and-pepper hair. Could he have been running from the scene of the crime? Was that why he didn't want his picture taken? She'd keep the information filed in her brain in case she needed to tell someone.

Molly inserted her key and turned the handle. Nothing. She banged on it. Sounds of locks being released came from the other side. The door cracked open. Hilga peered through a crack. "I have company. Come back later."

"It's my room, too." Molly glanced both ways down the hall. Her heart raced like the massive engines beneath them.

"Please?" Hilga opened the door a bit wider and gave a puppy dog look.

Gag! Couldn't the woman think of someone other than herself? Would Molly have to deal with this type of immorality the entire cruise?

"Fine." She stomped to the elevators and pushed the up button. She might as well take photos in the casino. Even if she was off the clock. It beats sitting around, waiting for her roommate to get her kicks and a killer to find her. If she couldn't stay locked in her cabin, then the next best place was a room full of people. Being alone on deck had been stupid. She could be shark bait right now.

The music of coins clanked in metal trays, winners shouted, and shrieking laughter rang. A loud, crazy place. She roamed the aisles and snapped photos of folks with their arms wrapped around buckets of silver. She was glad to see the cruise line hadn't progressed to paper tickets. The sound of winnings spilling out was a happy sound. One woman held the skirt of her dress beneath the slot machine's spout as quarters spilled over. Molly laughed as she snapped the photo.

The man she'd fallen on during dinner sat in the Keno section. Mr. Morrison, Lance called him. He rested his head in his hands. Molly veered in another direction. No way was she going to get in his way again. She moved upstairs to the lounge and glanced over the banister to people watch.

Her gaze locked with Lances' and she froze. The man had to be stalking her! She tried to keep from staring, but who could when her eyes rested on a man as handsome as a movie star. She shook her head. No time for love. She had work to do.

She smiled and stepped back to ask for a glass of water from the barmaid. Once she'd received her drink, she located an empty table, then sat and slipped off her shoes.

She glanced up from rubbing her feet. Robert sauntered in and chose a stool in front of the bar. Lance climbed the stairs soon after. His face split with a grin when he spotted Molly, and he strolled in her direction. The man was nothing if not persistent.

"You must be extremely bored." Molly twirled her glass in the puddle of condensation on the table.

"Why? Because I prefer the company of a beautiful woman to being alone?" Lance slid onto the seat across from her.

"Why me?"

"I'm intrigued. Your comment about needing a cop put every one of my instincts on edge."

Her nerves snapped to attention. She needed to get out of there. "I'm not a criminal!" Is that what he thought? "There are a number of reasons why I might need a police officer."

"I didn't say you were, but your actions are more suspicious now, than they were earlier." Lance lifted his hand to signal the waitress. "You can't leave a comment like that one hanging and not have me take the bait. If you'd hung around long enough, I could've told you I'm a cop."

Molly gnawed the inside of her cheek. Should she tell him? Antonio said they should keep it to themselves until they docked at the next port. She *should* have informed the captain. Could she get in trouble for not doing so? With a deep breath, she shoved her hand inside her camera bag and withdrew the picture.

"See anything suspicious?" She slid it across the table. The weight on her shoulders going along for the ride.

After a few moments to study it, Lance frowned. His piercing gaze clashed with hers. "Where did you get this?"

"I took it this morning." She tapped the image of a man's frame in the window. "Antonio, the photo tech, pointed that out to me during dinner."

Lord, let Lance be one of the good guys.

"Do others know?" He handed it back to her.

Molly shook her head and shoved the photo out of sight. "I'm afraid to tell anyone."

"Where did you take this?"

"In front of the warehouse before the ship sailed."

He stood. "Come on. We need to show this to the captain."

Her throat tightened. "I didn't know what to do, and I'm hiding from every man whose silhouette could possibly match that one. Antonio said he caught a glimpse of the side of the killer's face, and he has salt and pepper hair. He wore a polo shirt." Just like the rude man from earlier. She hesitated, not wanting to finish her thought, but he needed to know everything, if he was going to help her. She licked suddenly dry lips to moisten them. "And that he glanced at me when my camera's flash went off."

"We don't know for sure that anyone was killed."

Indignation colored her vision. Was he questioning her credibility? "Antonio saw the man fall to the floor."

"Why didn't he say something then?"

Molly shrugged. "He's probably scared."

"Let's talk to Antonio first. This should have gone straight to the captain before we set sail. Where is Antonio now?"

"Most likely his cabin. He's down the hall from me."

"Let's go."

"Passengers aren't allowed downstairs."

"If we're caught, I'll flash my badge and deal with the questions then."

Like an eager puppy, Molly followed, almost running to keep up with Lance's long strides. Having his arm in a sling didn't seem to slow him down any. Obviously, when the man was on a mission he had a one-track mind. She caught up, and out of the corner of her eye, noted his firm chin set like marble, the hard glint in his eye. Wait a minute! How did she know he was who he said he was? Maybe he was the killer. He didn't have salt and pepper hair, but he could've colored it.

She skidded to a halt. "Can I see some identification?"

"Excuse me?"

"You haven't proven to me that you're a police officer."

Lance rolled his eyes and pulled his badge from his pocket. "Satisfied?"

Molly inspected the engraved metal. "Is it real?"

"Yes. You can call the mainland and check if you'd like."

"I believe you."

Their quick pace continued until they stopped outside Antonio's cabin. Molly knocked. They waited a few seconds, and she knocked again. Lance reached across her and tried the door. It swung open. She felt the blood drain from her face to her toes. Noxious odors stung her nostrils. Nausea rose.

Antonio lay sprawled across one of the single beds with a plastic bag tied around his face.

CYNTHIA HICKEY

3

L ance rubbed a hand over his face. So much for a vacation. He'd landed smack dab in the middle of a murder investigation at sea. Unless Molly's camera had caught one on land as well. The first trickle of excitement ran down his spine. Who needed rest and relaxation anyway? "We definitely need to speak with the captain."

Molly nodded, tears welling in her eyes. "Poor Antonio." She turned. "I'll get Captain Barker."

"Okay. I'll make sure no one enters the room. No, wait!" Her back stiffened. The last thing Molly needed to do after snapping that photo was to wander the ship alone. "Call him. Under no circumstances should you be alone. Understand?"

Her lips tightened. "Yes." She moved to the phone on the wall. "This is Molly Nicholson. I need to speak with Captain Barker, please. I don't care where he is!" Her voice shrilled. "Send him to Antonio's cabin."

Lance placed a hand on Molly's shoulder. "Calm down. It'll be okay." He cringed at the lame, clichéd attempt at placating a hysterical woman.

She hung up the phone and slumped to the floor. Lance slid down beside her and placed his arm around her shoulders to pull her close. There was no denying the fact she felt good there. Soft, warm, and all female. But, he found himself at a loss. His former partner had always taken over in situations like this one. He missed her. He led Molly to a chair and lowered her into it as a red-faced man wearing a bathrobe burst into the room. "Stay here."

"I'm Captain Barker. What is so all-fired important?" His gaze swept the room and stopped on Antonio. "Oh." The captain released the word in a loud sigh, and he took a step back. "What's going on?"

Lance pulled his badge from his pocket. "Detective Lance Spencer. LAPD. Molly found him."

Captain Barker frowned. "Are you here on business?"

"No, it *was* a vacation." Until he'd decided to get to know a curly-haired blonde a little better. He'd always been a sucker for a pretty face, but nothing in his life prepared him for murder on a cruise ship. How different could it be?

Barker turned to Molly. "Miss Nicholson, please contact the chief purser, the doctor, and security. Keep it quiet. No need for the passengers to find out. Detective, perhaps you could explain in greater detail." He tightened the sash around his waist, hiding the sweat pants beneath.

Lance retrieved the photo from Molly's camera bag. "This was taken this morning by Miss Nicholson and printed by Antonio. We have no proof there was a murder committed on land, but there's no denying we're looking at one now."

"This has never happened on a Midnight Cruise before. Definitely not on the *Destiny*." The Captain glanced at the picture and returned it as if it might catch fire. "Could it be suicide?"

"Seriously?" Was the man for real? Lance raised his eyebrows. He'd heard of it before, but only extremely rare cases.

Captain Barker shook his head. "No. I'm grasping at straws. I can't believe we have a possible murder to deal with now."

Lance nodded. "I'm not sure what to do in regard to a crime at sea. Do we need to call the FBI?"

"They only have jurisdiction twelve miles from shore. We can get them involved if someone's killed in Hawaii. Otherwise, it's up to our senior vice president of security, or SVP as we call him, to wrap things up, along with the help of Hawaii's finest. We'll contact them at port."

Lance rolled his head, trying to remove the crick taking up residence between his shoulder blades. "I think if we notify the FBI of a possible murder stateside, they'll check into it and get involved. If for nothing else but to ask questions."

The captain sighed again. "And detain us." He straightened his shoulders. "Nothing to be done about it. The safety of the passengers comes first."

*

Molly choked down the threatening nausea. She'd barely kept it at bay since she'd seen Antonio's body, and kept her face averted while she followed the captain's orders and waited. She hung up and leaned back to listen to the two men's conversation. Staying longer on a Hawaiian Island didn't sound too bad to her.

The purser and SVP, both over six feet,one thin, the other burly, stepped into the room as if marching to a guillotine. The purser graying on the sides, while the SVP sported a military crew cut.

The captain greeted them with a stern look. "Business goes on as usual, folks. No need for those not directly involved to get wind of this."

The SVP, Jack Morley, pulled a master key from his pocket. "This cabin stays locked. Make up a story for Antonio's roommate, and he can bunk somewhere else. We need to question the other employees. We'll set up a staff meeting as soon as possible; see whether anyone saw anything." He shook his head. "I don't have the personnel for this."

"I'll help." Lance spoke up. "I've worked the homicide division for five years. I'll also personally keep Miss Nicholson in my sight. She could be in danger."

Molly's heart lurched. She took a deep breath. Lance's presence would make her feel safer. At least from someone else. In regard to him, he gazed at her as if he'd like to have her for dessert. Her face heated. Despite her protests, she didn't think spending a lot of time with Lance was a bad thing.

Exhaustion slammed her like a rogue wave. "Can I go to my cabin now?" She wanted nothing more than to escape the horrors of the day.

Lance nodded. "I'll take you. Gentlemen, I'll return once she's safely locked in her cabin."

Molly exited before him and set off at a quick pace. Her heels thudded against the carpeted floor. The empty corridor left her feeling exposed. On a ship that boasted of two employees for each passenger, the halls were usually difficult to traverse. Crew members flirted, rushed to their next post, tried to catch a quick nap, or rendezvous with their latest flame. Everything would change. Now, they'd be looking over their shoulders for a murderer.

Lance towered over her. She felt safety in his presence. She stopped in front of her cabin, turned, hand gripping the doorknob. "Thank you."

His hand shot out to stop her. "Don't open the door for anyone but your roommate. Keep it locked. She has a key she can use to get in. I should check the room before you enter."

"Okay." She paused. What if Hilga had company again? She knocked, then pushed the door open when no one answered. "It's fine. Thanks again." She stepped inside, closed and locked it behind her before Lance could catch sight of the mess Hilga'd left. Her gaze scanned the cramped space. Piles of Hilga's clothes littered the floor. Makeup bottles cluttered the dresser. Cheap perfume vapors filled the air.

Nowhere for anyone to hide, other than the shower. She should've asked Lance to check for her. She shoved aside the cream-colored vinyl curtain. Empty. A sob caught her throat.

After placing her camera bag on the dresser, Molly fell across her bed and allowed the tears she'd held in to have full rein. Her first day on the job and her only friend onboard, brutally murdered. Photography was supposed to be a safe occupation!

Lord, what have I gotten myself into? Poor Antonio. All he cared about was living the high-life, making some money, and chasing women.

She couldn't get the image of his swollen face out of her mind. Grabbing her pillow, Molly smashed it over her face. Maybe she should ask the ship's doctor for a sleeping aid. Anything to wipe away the image.

The door handle jiggled, then someone banged on the other side. Molly sat up with a shriek.

"Molly! Why's the door locked? Let me in." Hilga's irate German tone alerted Molly to her irritation. She obviously hadn't heard about Antonio. Or maybe she had and panicked as she tried to get in.

"Are you alone?" Molly pressed her face against the wood.

"Yes."

"Are you sure?"

"What is going on? Stop asking questions and let me in."

After letting her in, she quickly relocked the door. "Did you hear about Antonio?"

Hilga started unbuttoning her shirt. "No." She let her uniform fall to the floor and stepped into the bathroom. "What'd he do now?"

"Someone killed him."

Hilga peered around the corner. "What?"

"Smothered. With a plastic bag. I'm sure you'll find out in the morning. There's going to be a meeting." Molly flopped back onto her bed. "We aren't supposed to go anywhere alone."

"Why would we be in any danger? I'm a waitress. Besides serving food, and spending time with my fling of the week, I mind my own business. He just broke up with his girlfriend. Maybe he did it himself. You said you had a bad breakup. Wouldn't be hard for you to understand how he might feel." She disappeared and the shower turned on.

"With a bag? Come on." Molly stared out the window. Waves lapped the horizon, silver beneath a full moon. Peaceful. Romantic. Trapping them in a floating hotel of death.

Hilga reappeared. "I've heard of stranger ways of knocking yourself off."

Molly contemplated telling her roommate about the picture, then decided against it. The less people who knew the better. Hilga could have a flippant attitude, but Molly knew she was in danger. Besides Antonio, Lance, and now the captain and security, she was the only one to set eyes on the infamous photograph.

God help her.

The killer could be anyone. How certain was she that the person had graying hair? He could've worn a wig. She gasped. Lance had shown up after the supposed murder. Maybe his act of concerned cop was exactly that. An act. What if a cold-blooded murderer lurked behind a handsome face and a badge?

Her heart threatened to burst from her chest. Who could she rely on? Empty-headed Hilga? Not likely. The captain? He'd be too busy. She was going to have to face the danger on her own.

Wait. She'd heard something in church about God protecting his children. Why hadn't she paid closer attention? If He did protect his children, then why were two people dead? Antonio had been Catholic. Didn't that count?

Her stomach churned and she bolted from the bed to pound on the bathroom door. "I need in."

"It's open," Hilga called.

Molly slammed through and lost her meager dinner in the toilet. Fear rippled across her skin. Lance's face flickered in her mind. She'd have to trust him.

There wasn't anyone else. *Lord, let him be who he*

says he is. Please.

"Are you sick?" Hilga stepped from the shower with a towel wrapped around her body. "Do you want me to call the doctor?"

The doctor couldn't cure what ailed her. Molly didn't think there was a pill made to take away the overwhelming feeling of terror.

4

Molly leaned on the railing and stared at the lush landscape of Kauai, Hawaii. Two police officers waited on the dock. Once the boat anchored, the gangplank was lowered. The men strode up the plank and on board. How could they hide this from the passengers now? A day on the island of Kauai would be delayed. With a sigh, she pushed away from the white rails and headed to breakfast.

Her hard-soled shoes slapped against the polished wood deck. Each slap echoed the guilty thoughts running rampant in her head. Antonio's death was her fault. She should have said something sooner. Why had she listened to him and waited? Was the killer watching her now? Icy fingernails raked down her spine. Molly stopped short of the restaurant door. Swallowing the sand dune in her throat, she glanced over her shoulder.

Those who strolled along the hallway paid no attention to her. Everyone's eyes were focused on something or someone else. Warmth seeped through her blood stream. She had no idea what the killer looked like except for her suspicion of salt-and-pepper hair. Which described half the male population on the ship. What if she were wrong? What if Antonio got the hair color wrong? It could be anyone!

The door swished open. A draft brought the tantalizing aroma of eggs, crepes, sausage, and ripe fruit. Molly barely had time to savor the smell before Lance's pinched face shoved into her view.

"I thought we agreed you wouldn't go anywhere alone." Lance held open the door. "We may be on a ship, but it took me forever to find you."

"I don't want to be a prisoner." She brushed past him, catching a whiff of his woodsy cologne. Great. The man smelled as good as he looked.

"The police would like to speak with you." He fell into step beside her. "They're in the security office."

She should be snapping photos, not being interrogated. Recording pleasant memories was what they had hired her to do. Her stomach plummeted the closer they got to security. The hallway she traversed felt like the proverbial green mile. Not that she'd been there, but she'd read about it. Seen it in movies. Perspiration threatened beneath her arms, and she crooked her elbows into slight wings to encourage air circulation. Why had she chosen the navy blue polo shirt today? It showed everything.

"Relax." Lance placed a hand on the small of her back. "You've done nothing wrong. They'll question us. Take a look at the photograph, question the employees who have cabins close to Antonio's, then tape off his room. We'll be free to go."

She glanced up at him. "That sounds too easy."

He flashed a grin that threatened to stop her heart. "I've volunteered to keep an open eye during the investigation. Most of the passengers think I'm just one of them. The only ones aware that I'm a detective are the top security man, SVP, and the captain. Maybe I'll hear something. And, I get to spend time with you."

Wow. She didn't know what to make of that last statement. Why would a man who'd just met her be so interested in a short, skinny woman with hair that wouldn't behave? Especially with a boat full of gorgeous women at his disposal. She had to work hours to get a tan, and she had freckles scattered across her face. She might be a child of English immigrants, but somewhere down the line an ancestor had been Irish. She was definitely not a picture of glamour. "Do I really need a bodyguard?"

"Do you want to take that chance?"

Endure his constant presence or chance a run-in with a faceless killer alone? The icy fingernails on her spine were back. No competition there. "No."

She shoved open the door to the security office. Except for their round, tanned faces, dark hair and eyes, the two officers didn't look anything like the actors on the old drama Hawaii 5-0. She wished they did. They'd be more welcoming. Instead, their stern faces caused her to break out into a sweat.

"I'm Officer Okymoto, this is Officer Brown. Please have a seat Miss Nicholson."

Molly perched on the edge of a hard plastic chair and clasped her moist hands in her lap.

"May I have the photograph?" Officer Okymoto held out his hand.

Pulling the picture from her camera case, Molly handed it over.

Several drawn out minutes passed while he studied it, and then handed it to Officer Brown. "We'll keep this. Any idea who the two men in the window are?"

Molly shook her head. "I didn't notice them until

Antonio developed the picture."

"And you found Mr. Rodriquez?"

Images of Antonio's bluish face flashed through her head. She winced, fighting them off. "Lance and I did."

Officer Okymoto jotted down her answers on a large yellow legal pad. "Why were you in his room?"

"I found out Lance was a police officer." Molly stared at the man's hand as it glided across the page. "I showed him the picture, and he wanted to speak to Antonio."

"Did you see anyone else?"

"No. The halls were empty, but most of the employees were either working, or enjoying some free time."

"We'll be questioning the other employees before releasing the ship." He cupped his fingers and rested them on his chin. "I've checked the crime scene, but doubt we'll come up with any clues. Crimes at sea are difficult to solve. Detective Spencer will continue to investigate during the cruise. Unofficially, of course."

"Can I continue with my job?" Lord, don't let them fire her. She didn't have the funds to fly back home. She'd taken the photography job to make some easy money in a fun way and to have the opportunity to see exotic locations. Not to mention getting over the heartache of an abusive relationship.

"Under the supervision of Detective Spencer. The perpetrator likely knows you took this photograph. We don't want you taking any chances." Officer Okymoto stood and directed his comments to the captain. "Give us a couple of hours to finish here, and we'll clear the ship."

That was it? Molly's shoulders slumped. Wasn't the

ship a part of the United States? Didn't the passengers and the victim warrant the same consideration that a murder on the mainland would receive? She'd heard stories about crimes at sea and the rushed investigations done, but she'd written them off as rumors.

Molly rose. "What about the FBI?"

Okymoto frowned. "We'll know more after our investigation, Miss Nicholson. Let us do our job, and you continue doing yours." The two officers marched from the room.

Summarily dismissed and feeling like a 'little' woman who'd been put in her place, Molly's face heated. "Of all the arrogant, self-righteous … "

"That's enough, Miss Nicholson." The captain's reprimand made her stiffen. "You have a job to do. I'm sure there are still passengers at breakfast. They'll have questions. Answer as little as possible." He skirted the edge of the security officer's desk. "Keep them happy."

Lance grasped her hand. With a nod to the captain, he led her from the room.

Once out of sight, she jerked free of his hold and adopted a mocking look on her face, complete with pruned lips. "Now, be a good little girl and do as you're told. Keep your mouth shut, and let the men handle things." Her fists clenched. "The man might as well have spoken those exact words. Ugh!"

A bemused look passed over Lance's face. He placed a hand on her shoulder, kneading the knot forming at the base of her neck. "You need some down time."

"I have a few hours this afternoon." His massage made it hard to concentrate. It was especially difficult to hold onto a bad mood.

She pasted on her required happy face. Marching down the hall and up two flights of stairs, she kept her chin up and spine straight. Once they reached the dining room, she took a deep breath, lifted her camera, and began to take pictures of those still left in the room.

"Want to visit the island with me?" Lance wiggled his eyebrows.

Despite her irritation at being treated in what she perceived as a chauvinistic manner by the police, she smiled. "I'd love to. I've heard of this great cave we can check out. Oh, wait. Wrong island. But this one has a lighthouse."

"Will the cave be dark?" He winked.

"They do advise flashlights." She laughed at the impish look on his face. "You, Mr. Spencer, are a flirt."

"Makes life more interesting."

Oh, boy.

*

Stretched out in a lounge chair beside the pool, Lance kept an eye on Molly while she flitted from passenger to passenger snapping pictures. Trim legs flashed beneath white shorts. A simple blue tee-shirt and red belt completed the ensemble. He wished for a camera of his own. Someone ought to take her picture.

"Do you know why we're not allowed on shore yet?" A plump woman fell into the chair next to him, almost knocking him over with a sweet wave of perfume wafting from her. "I went on this cruise to see the islands."

"No, ma'am." Lance pulled a pair of sunglasses from his pocket. Isn't that why everyone took a Hawaiian cruise?

She leaned closer and lowered her voice. "I heard

one of the crew members was murdered last night. Awful thing. Then someone else said he killed himself because of a broken heart. I wonder which it was."

"You shouldn't believe everything you hear." Lance laid his head back and pretended to sleep. News traveled fast. When he found out who leaked the information, he'd strangle them. The woman's cloying perfume threatened to gag him. He turned his head away.

"Well, my roommate heard it from one of the waitresses. So it must be true. They're like a close-knit family, the crew members. They wouldn't make up something so terrible if it weren't true."

"Uh-huh." Thankful the glasses hid his eyes, he kept his gaze focused on Molly. A man approached her, said something that made her hang her head, then she moved on, taking pictures.

Molly weaved her way through the throng of sunbathers to Lance's side. "That was Antonio's roommate. He said the boat has been cleared. They're lowering the gangplank as we speak."

The lady next to him sat up with a gleeful shriek, clapped her hands, and bolted from her chair. "Wonderful."

Lance sat up and pulled Molly away from the woman's prying ears. "Let's do some sightseeing."

"Shouldn't you do some investigating first?"

"No. You're my first priority. Investigating is second. The local police have jurisdiction here. I'm just to inform them if I find out anything. I'm on vacation, remember?"

"So you say."

"Detective Spencer?" Lance turned at Officer

Okymoto's voice. "As suspected, we've found nothing. A few prints, but I'm willing to bet they belong to the cabin occupants or cleaning crew. We contacted Honolulu. A body was found early this morning in the empty warehouse beside the dock. Looks like a routine mugging."

"ID?"

Okymoto shook his head. "Not yet."

Lance glanced down into Molly's pale face. "Was he strangled?"

The Officer nodded. "You may be right about Miss Nicholson being in danger. The SVP will help watch out for her and continue to search the ship for clues. We have no reason to detain the passengers any longer. We don't know that the murderer is on board. Most likely he fled the area as soon as the gangplank was lowered. But, mind you, we haven't completely ruled out suicide."

"I'll have the captain inform me if any scheduled arrivals on board fail to show each evening." Lance shook the officer's hand. If Antonio committed suicide, he'd eat a volcanic rock.

Guiding Molly from the deck, he felt her tremble beneath his hand. "Are you all right?"

She nodded. "I've never been in danger before for anything worse than a broken heart. Maybe a bruise or two." A shaky laugh escaped her. "And I've had plenty of those."

"Here." Lance lowered her into a plush chair in the lounge. "Relax for a minute. We'll leave when most of the passengers have gone."

"I need to pray." Molly lowered her head.

Lance took her hands in his. She glanced up, a

surprised look on her face, then bowed her head again before praying silently. Lance sat in agreement with her as his gaze roamed the crowd waiting to disembark. He didn't agree with Okymoto's assessment of the culprit fleeing the ship. Where better to hide than in plain sight? Which one of the passengers or crew was a cold-blooded killer?

5

This will be great." Molly flashed Lance a grin and waved a tourist brochure in his face. "There's lots to see on Kauai. On all the islands, actually. Maybe I'll take an Alaskan cruise next. Or the Mediterranean. I could ship hop for the rest of my life."

His returned smile caused her heart to flip-flop, and her eyes dropped to his chiseled lips. She wrenched her gaze away before he caught her staring.

"I've rented a car. Where do you want to go first?" His smile widened.

Apparently he could decipher what she'd been thinking. The cad.

A car? She'd expected a tour bus. A car was much better. "How about we start on the north shore and work our way back to the ship? There's something to see around every corner. There's a lighthouse I want to visit, and a chanting beach. Wouldn't it be cool to shout Bible verses across the waves?" She motioned to her camera. "If I see passengers, I'll snap some great shots and get mementos of my own in the meantime. What about you? Anything in particular?"

"Nope. I'm sure whatever you want will be fine with me."

She scowled. There were about a million questions

she wanted to ask. Once they were in the car, away from hundreds of pairs of ears, she would fire away. Vacation, her foot! Something else was behind Lance's motive for taking a cruise, and she intended to find out what.

"I'll choose where we eat lunch." Lance winked.

"Deal." Molly offered her arm.

Lance intertwined his arm with hers, and they merged with the crowd of sightseers heading down the gangplank and on shore.

Hawaiian girls stood with arms weighted down by heavy scented leis. Molly bowed her head to allow the circle of orchids to be put around her neck, then stood to the side while the welcoming committee greeted Lance.

Lush flowers in every hue of the rainbow dotted the landscape of the island. Their heavy fragrance teased her nose, inching its way through her body. Molly closed her eyes and inhaled the smell of jasmine, orchids, and other tropical plants. Her spirits lifted, helping her forget the gruesome sight of Antonio's lifeless body. Nothing would spoil this day. She lifted her chin. There wasn't anything she couldn't accomplish when she set her mind to it.

A navy-blue Mustang convertible was parked not far away. An attendant clad in a turquoise floral print shirt and khaki shorts stood guard. Lance showed identification and took the offered keys.

Molly slid into the front seat and giggled at his frown. Maybe she should've waited for him to open the door for her. Tough. They weren't on a date. She was a semi-tourist slash photographer and he was her bodyguard. Nothing more.

Within minutes they were on a road curving around the island. The thick green foliage rose on one side of them, on the other the brilliant ocean twinkled in the sunlight, hurting her eyes. Definitely heaven come to earth.

Molly tore her attention away from the scenery. No sense beating around the bush. Surprise would be her best attack. "Why are you really on this cruise?"

The only indication that her question bothered him was a tightening of his grip on the steering wheel. "Excuse me?" He cut his gaze to her.

"You're too willing to give up your vacation to follow me around." She crossed her arms. "Sure, you're a cop, but you aren't active right now, right? This isn't about my unpaid parking tickets is it?"

His laugh rang out. "No, this isn't about that. Although you should pay them."

"I will." She tilted her head. "As soon as I have the money. Now answer my question."

"Okay." He shrugged his good shoulder. "It's no secret. My supervisor ordered it."

"Why?"

His cheeks puffed with a sigh. "I was wounded on the job. My partner was killed." He paused and a muscle ticked in his jaw. His eyes shimmered, and he sniffed. His voice lowered to a husky growl. "I was told to take some time off. I'd never been on a cruise. Always wanted to see Hawaii. So here I am." A dimple winked next to his mouth. "I found myself bored before the ship left Honolulu."

"How can you be bored on a cruise?"

"I'm not much of a party person, and you won't find me taking a pottery class or water aerobics."

She nodded. Her ex had been the opposite. Partying until all hours of the night, calling her to pick him up because he'd drank too much.

"So landing in the middle of a murder investigation spiced things up." Molly crossed her arms and stared back at the passing greenery. "Glad I could oblige."

"The view isn't bad either."

"It is gorgeous."

"No argument there."

The deepening of his voice dragged her attention back to him. The heated look he slid her way made her cheeks flame. He wasn't talking about the incredible sights around them. Suddenly self-conscious, she uncrossed her arms and clasped her hands in her lap.

He wiggled his eyebrows.

She laughed. "Stop doing that."

"Why?"

"It makes you look like a little boy. A bad little boy." And that was the last thing she needed. Or wanted. The man's charm could suck her in faster than a giant whirlpool. A relationship was not on the agenda. She spotted their first destination. "Oh, look!"

A red and white lighthouse rose stark and simple on an emerald peninsula. An azure sea and clear sky provided a striking background. She flipped through the brochure. "The fifty-two foot Kilauea Lighthouse was erected in 1913. Its beam once reached ninety miles out to sea." She took a deep breath. "Wouldn't that have been romantic? A woman standing in that spot at the end, waiting for the ship her lover worked on to return."

"Yep."

She rolled her eyes. A one word answer for something so glorious. Men.

Lance stopped the car and she shoved her door open, and bounded out, camera still slung around her neck. The sun's rays kissed her face. Using the lighthouse as the focal point, Molly snapped a photo, then turned to the tourists milling about. She recognized some of the faces and spent a few minutes doing her job.

"Can't you let me at least pretend to be a gentleman?" The close proximity of Lance sent her in a frenzy of alert nerve endings and hyperactive senses. How could one man cause such chaos?

Swallowing, she inched over a step. The ocean wind blew away the scent of his cologne. "Sorry. What would you like to do?"

He focused the full power of his coffee-colored eyes on her. "I'm talking about opening car doors for you. Maybe carrying your camera or the equipment? It looks heavy."

"Sorry to offend your sensibilities. I'm used to doing for myself." She stared at the lighthouse to avoid his gaze. "The camera isn't as heavy as it looks. Come on, let's get a closer look."

Molly headed for the tourist entrance, paused, and faced Lance. She flashed a sly smile at him. "If you're feeling chivalrous, you could pay my parking tickets."

*

Lance couldn't deny it. Her enthusiasm was contagious. He grinned as she grabbed his hand and tugged him closer to the lighthouse.

"Let's climb to the top."

He glanced up, not relishing the strenuous activity. At least he hadn't been shot in the leg. Or dead like Abigail. Suddenly his troubles seemed miniscule in comparison.

His gaze traveled upward, imagining her looking down from heaven as his personal guardian angel. He sighed and let his gaze rest again on the lighthouse. It rose as tall as Jack's beanstalk. He swallowed against the lump rising in his throat.

By the time they reached the top, they both breathed heavily. Molly took pictures around the metal grate protecting the lamp. Lance glanced over the edge, his breath seized, and he stepped back. Did the woman have no fear? What if the grate broke? She would plummet to her death and he could do nothing to prevent it.

He swallowed against the lump in his throat. "Can we go back down?" Why did he sound like a boy going through puberty? He cleared his throat.

"Are you afraid of heights?"

"No." Yes. In the worst way.

She turned and studied his face. "You are! Why didn't you say something? I could've climbed up alone."

"I thought I could handle it."

"I guess gazing off the point out there is out of the question. It's a sheer drop to the ocean. You can hear the surf from here. Lots of big rocks jutting—"

"That's enough." Perspiration broke out on his upper lip. He grasped her elbow and pulled her toward the stairs. "We passed an outdoor flea market about a half mile back. Let me buy you lunch." That should be safe enough. Away from towering cliffs and buildings that touched the sky.

He hefted her equipment bag and motioned for her to lead the way to the car. The breeze carried a whiff of her perfume. Something light, floral, and completely feminine.

She stood primly beside the car door, her lips curled in a Mona Lisa smile, while she waited for him to be chivalrous and open the door. He chuckled and placed the bag in the back seat before reaching for the handle.

The wind across his face as they drove erased the tension of the lighthouse. He pulled up to the market and rolled his head on his neck. Molly still grinned at him. The minx. Obviously it made her feel good to know he had a weakness. "You are an evil woman."

"And you said you'd feed me. I'm hungry."

"Ever had taro leaves wrapped around rice?"

"No, and I'm not trying poi. I don't eat purple food. You said you've never been to Hawaii."

"I haven't. My partner brought me back some once. That and fresh pineapple. We'll feast on both today."

The smile she rewarded him was worth another bullet. They approached the first vendor, made their purchases, and bit in.

Molly's eyes widened. "It's sweet rice. Honey?"

He nodded. "Yes, dear."

"Oh, you're a comedian!" She took another bite. "When we're finished here, I want to buy some souvenirs. I've always wanted a muumuu."

"That's something I wouldn't have expected." The dress would dwarf her small frame. He could better picture her in a grass skirt. His comfort level around her surprised him. When Abigail died, he'd sworn off women. Forever, he thought. It'd taken a couple of weeks to realize the love he'd felt for Abby was more like a brother to a sister. Still, her death cut him with razors.

"Tell me about your partner. What kind of a guy was he?"

Molly's inquiry surfaced emotions he thought he'd moved past. He didn't talk much about that day, or Abby's death. One reason his boss ordered the vacation time. The department shrink refused to clear him for duty until he took some R&R. Lance drew in a deep breath and released it slowly. He could do this.

"Her. My partner's name was Abigail. Abby." He led the way to a wooden picnic table. "And she was wonderful. Smart, beautiful, and brave. My best friend." The memory still made his heart ache. "She was killed by the man who shot me. We were called to a routine domestic violence. Nothing unusual in a town the size I work for. It turned out to be anything but. She should've been off duty, but I talked her into one more call."

Silence hung over them like the humid tropic air. Molly glanced down at her food. "You loved her."

He took a deep breath and released it in a way that puffed out his cheeks. "Of course. Like a sister. But we wouldn't have worked as a couple. She was too independent, and I'm too stubborn."

"Love covers a multitude of sins." She shrugged. "Or so they say."

"Spoken like a true jilted woman."

She nodded. "Yes. I chose a handsome, self-centered, supposedly Christian man. To use your words, he was anything but." A shadow passed over her eyes. Molly squared her shoulders. "Turned out my love for him was nothing more than infatuation, and his love for himself was larger than his love for God. I'm smarter now."

"But he's the reason you took a job on a cruise ship." Lance wiped his hand on a napkin and readjusted his sling.

"Correct again."

"Doesn't sound like you're completely over him."

"I am." She gave him a tight lipped smile and turned to throw their garbage in the nearest trash receptacle.

A young man leaped from behind a tree and grabbed the strap to Molly's camera bag. Her neck snapped to the side as her feet flew out from beneath her.

CYNTHIA HICKEY

6

Molly's neck jerked to the side like it would be disconnected from her shoulders. Before she knew it, she found herself flat on her back with a pounding headache and the breath knocked from her. She stared into a sapphire sky. Afternoon rain misted her face.

Lance bent over her, his face a mask of anxiety. He waved back the circle of strangers flocking around them. "Are you all right?"

"My camera." She felt for it, reassured to find it still around her neck. "Why didn't you go after him?" She pushed to a sitting position.

"That would've entailed leaving you here alone." Lance tilted her face to his and peered into her eyes. "How many fingers am I holding up?"

"Two." She slapped his hand away.

Lance sighed. "He didn't get anything. Don't move. Your head hit a rock, and I think you blacked out for a minute. I need to get you to the ship's doctor. An ambulance is on its way."

"I'm fine. I'm not riding in an ambulance." She waved him away and tried to stand. "You can take me back as well as anyone." She blinked against the black fuzzy outline around his face. Her legs refused to cooperate, and she crumpled in a heap.

"Don't be so stubborn." Lance shrugged off his sling and swept her in his arms.

"Your shoulder." Why couldn't she hold her head up? She put a hand to the back of her neck. A lump the size of a golf ball had taken up residence. Her stomach churned like the ocean during a hurricane.

His chest rumbled beneath her ear as he said something she couldn't decipher. "I'm fine," she repeated. The world grew fuzzy, and she closed her eyes.

When she opened them, they were whipping around the roads of Kauai like a NASCAR driver. Her simple lunch threatened to escape. She didn't relish the flight over the cliffs, and the speed did nothing for her head or the nausea. "If you don't slow down, we'll be going swimming."

"Oh, good, you're awake. You scared me." He spared her a glance and focused back on his driving. "How's your neck? You've got a welt where the camera strap rubbed it. I shouldn't have let you talk me into driving you."

Molly pressed her head against the headrest and tried not to move. By the way the words spewed from his mouth, Lance was concerned. But, a welt was the least of her worries. Losing her lunch topped the list. She closed her eyes against the tears threatening to spill. When had she turned into such a weeping Wendy? It seemed like she wanted to cry at least once an hour lately.

That boy could've stolen her camera bag. More than a home for the tools of her trade, she used it as a purse. It contained all of her identification. That could've resulted in her being fired. Well, maybe not. But she'd spent the last of her money on the Nikon, and didn't want to use one issued by the ship. She knew this one's quirks.

"Why did somebody want my camera? To sell?"

"Maybe."

"You don't think so?"

"I'll see about getting the photos printed while the doctor examines you."

Oh. She understood now. Somebody thought she had something incriminating on her camera. Her skin prickled. Clips of pictures she'd taken since dropping her card off with Antonio flickered through her mind. All the photos were of passengers and scenery, which meant … "I could have a picture of the killer again."

Lance nodded. "I want to compare what you have now with the one you took yesterday. Maybe we'll have a face for the authorities to run through the database."

Then they could put an end to the nightmare. *Please, God, let it be so.*

*

When Lance saw the thug pull Molly to the ground, he thought his heart had stopped. History threatened to repeat itself. After the kid failed to get the bag, he'd disappeared in the mass of people at the flea market. It could have been much worse. Time to get his weapon out of his suitcase.

Despite the throbbing in his shoulder, he insisted on carrying Molly onboard and setting her on a sofa until someone retrieved a wheelchair. Her paleness left him weak in the knees, and his heart rate sporadic.

The ship's doctor, Max Duncan, a man who matched Lance in height, arrived with a wheel chair.

"This is a little different than the sea sickness or sprained ankles I usually get." He knelt beside Molly. "Molly, I'm going to help you into the chair. Let me know if you feel like you're going to pass out."

"I'm fine."

"She keeps saying that." Lance rubbed a hand over her face. "And I think I pulled a stitch carrying her in here."

"I'll take a look at you next. Where can I contact you?"

He removed the camera bag from around Molly's neck. "Photography."

Max raised his eyebrows, but said nothing as he wheeled Molly into the elevator. Knowing that she'd be okay under the doctor's care, Lance waved when she opened her eyes long enough to spear him with a look. He laughed, knowing she'd rather go with him than be poked and prodded by the doctor. "I'll be right back," he told her.

Once the doors closed, he turned toward the service part of the ship. With most of the passengers on shore, the halls were empty. Inside the lab, a young man he hadn't met lounged in a chair reading an automotive magazine with his feet propped on the developing machine. "How long until you can get these developed?"

The boy's feet clunked to the floor. "An hour tops. You're the cop that's helping security find Antonio's killer, right?"

Lance rolled his shoulders. He would've liked to have kept his identity a secret from most of the passengers and crew. "Word gets around."

"Especially among the crew on a ship. We have few

secrets. It can be good or bad." The young man's teeth flashed brilliant against his ebony skin. "I'm Mahamud. These photos will be my top priority."

"I'll be in the clinic." Lance marched from the room. Having most, if not all, the crew knowing who he was would not help him uncover information undetected. His steps quickened. He wanted to be with Molly when the photos were developed. They'd study them together. If she felt up to it.

He pushed open the door to the clinic as Max taped a bandage to the back of Molly's head. He glanced up. "She has a concussion. Not a bad one, but I'd advise rest for the next day or two."

She pushed his hand away. "I have a job to do."

"I'll inform the captain and the purser of my assessment. They'll agree with me." Max restored his supplies in a cabinet and locked it. "You, little lady, seem to have attracted the attention of an unwanted admirer, for lack of a better word. Take my advice and enjoy the rest of the cruise with the detective here. Your injuries weren't your fault."

There wasn't anything Lance would enjoy more than spending time with the feisty Molly. He didn't know for sure why the information pleased him so much, but spending the next week with Molly brightened his day. "Can she walk?"

"Sure. I've given her something for the nausea and pain." He waved at the other examining table. "Now, let me look at your shoulder."

Max helped Lance out of his shirt, then removed his dressing. "Just pulled a little. No harm done. You can probably do without the sling at least half the day. Start regaining use of that arm."

"Thanks."

When the doctor's work was completed, Lance helped Molly to her feet. "Let's sit on the deck for a while."

"Did you turn in the photos?"

"Should be done within the next thirty minutes."

Keeping the pace slow, he led her to the upper deck. With Molly settled onto a white lounge chair, he took the one next to her. The ocean breeze blew blond strands into her eyes and Lance stretched over to tuck it behind her ear. Like silk. Her color had returned, replacing her previous look of marble to one of a pink rose. He settled back and crossed his arms.

God, I'd like to know what you're doing. The plans for an onboard, harmless flirtation weren't panning out as he'd planned. Instead, the woman next to him jumbled his emotions. It wasn't just the fact she could be a target that made him want to spend all his time with her. It was her. The graceful way she moved. How easily laughter bubbled past her defenses. And the haunted look in her eyes that made him want to kiss it away.

His gaze slid from the beauty of the island rising beside the ship, to Molly. She'd fallen asleep. Long lashes cast shadows on her cheeks. Her lips parted slightly, inviting him to lean in for a kiss. He dragged in a deep breath and averted his eyes. He had it bad. All the stories he scorned of love at first sight, and the bug had taken a big bite out of him. What would they do when the ship reached Vancouver?

"Here you go." Mahamud appeared at his side. "I rushed them through."

Lance straightened and took the large manila

envelope. "Thanks. Molly, the photos are here." He pulled out the fistful of photos and handed them to her, then withdrew the rest. Molly was a talented photographer, catching the subject's personality. His favorites were the candid shots. The passengers would be forking over a lot of their cash to purchase these. He perused photo after photo and found nothing incriminating.

Molly waved a photo in front of his face. "Look."

Taken from the top of the lighthouse, she'd captured the profile of a man below. He appeared to be staring up at them; half his face covered by shadow.

"I'm thinking if we blew that up," a smile spread across her face. "We'd see the same profile as in the warehouse picture."

7

It might be a long shot, but Molly felt sure the man in the photo was the same as the person in the photo from the previous day. She swung her legs over the side of the chair. "Let's take it to the lab."

Lance's hand shot out. "Slow down. You're supposed to be taking it easy."

"I took a nap. How much easier can I take it?"

"Fifteen minutes does not constitute a nap."

"For you maybe." She stood. Her head swam, and she gripped the back of the chaise to hide her discomfort. No way would he let her go if he knew she still got dizzy. Lifting her chin, she stared him down. "Are you coming or am I going alone?" She knew that would get him. If nothing else, Lance Spencer took his job seriously. Whether it was a volunteer one or not.

His brows drew together. "Woman, you're going to be the death of me."

She refused to be intimidated and met his glare, dead on, almost sinking into the dark warmth of his eyes. A lump rose in her throat. Swallowing, she forced it away. "That's very possible." The thought sent a chill down her spine. The knowledge that assuming the role of her bodyguard might cause danger to Lance did not sit well with her. He already occupied entirely too much of her thoughts. Besides, she couldn't have feelings for someone after two days. Right?

He towered over her. "Don't think scowling at me will convince me your head isn't hurting."

In order to prevent jarring her pounding head, Molly took measured steps as she led the way back to the lab. The lab stood empty. Daniella was obviously out taking photos. Maybe Mahamud, the other tech, was on break. The crew had little time to themselves while at sea. They took the time when they could get it. Molly sighed. Here she was, on medical leave, her second day on the job. Her absence forced the others to take up the slack. If her recuperation time took too long, they might put her on the first flight home.

When Lance joined her, he closed the door behind them. "Can you blow it up?"

Pulled away from her pity party, she nodded. "Yes. The photographers, as well as the lab techs, are trained on the equipment."

Lance leaned close while she worked. His cologne masked the astringent odor emanating from the developing machine. His breath stirred the hairs on the back of her neck, making her skin tingle. Her heart thumped with the rhythm of the machine. Goodness, the man oozed masculinity.

Despite the distraction of Lance, within ten minutes they stared at an enlarged, fuzzy image of a man's profile. Lance bent over the photo. "That could be Robert Morrison."

"He's our man." Molly wanted to laugh. It'd been so easy.

"Not necessarily. We don't have proof he killed anybody." He pulled the first photo out of his pocket and compared the two. "I repeat, *it could be*. The first picture is too dark to make an accurate statement. And we've lost a lot of clarity by blowing this one up."

Undeterred, Molly yanked the glossy paper away from him. "Then we'll have to watch him. Draw him out."

"You mean spy."

She shrugged. "Whatever it takes. Are you going to give this to security?"

"Yes. And have a copy sent to the Honolulu PD. They can run a background check on the guy."

"What do we do in the meantime?"

"Dinner, maybe?"

Her stomach growled. Her face heated as Lance chuckled. "Sounds good. I'm not sure I'll be able to resort to being a passenger. My fingers are already itching to take more photos. Maybe we could eat in the crew mess? Something light?"

He placed a hand on her lower back and guided her from the room. "Tomorrow. Today, you rest. Doctor's orders. And I don't think the crew would appreciate me intruding on their space."

Rest. She'd never done 'nothing' in her entire life. "Fine. But I want to sit at Morrison's table."

"Keep your mouth shut if we do."

"We'll see." Her skin rippled where his hand lay. What would it be like to be held by him? Not the 'I'm carrying you to safety' thing, although that had been nice, but a romantic embrace. Heavenly, she'd guess. But he'd have to lose the heavy-handed attitude. His good looks wouldn't persuade her to be bossed around for long.

When they reached the dining room, Lance settled

her into a chair and chose the seat next to her. "We probably should have had your dinner taken to your room. How bad does your head hurt?"

"A little. I'll go after I eat." She glanced around for Morrison. There was no sign of his salt-and-pepper hair and boxy frame. What if he didn't get back on board? Docking would've given him the perfect opportunity to make a run for it. It would have also cast more suspicion. The clock on the wall, and the subtle movement of the ship, told her they'd set sail. Her shoulders slumped. "Maybe you're right. I'll take something in my room."

Lance rose. "Let me get you settled, then I'll fill you a plate from the buffet."

"I'm really sorry to be such a bother."

Morrison entered the dining room and made straight for the buffet line.

"Oh, there he is!" she whispered. "I'll stay now."

"Absolutely not. I'll go to the captain if I have to." Lance's stern look convinced her he wouldn't be coerced. "And tell the chief purser."

"Okay. But you need to keep an eye on him."

"I promise."

*

She was the most exasperating woman he'd ever met. By the time he'd gotten past her bulldog of a roommate who stated, "Crew members are not permitted to fraternize with the passengers", flashed his badge, and had Molly safely ensconced in her room, fed, and promising to stay put, Lance felt as if he'd run a mile. He understood her enthusiasm in helping solve the crime, but there was a proper way to do it, and then there was the wrong way. Jumping in headfirst would only get her killed. He refused to live with the guilt of losing two women on his watch.

By the time he returned to the dining room, Morrison had left. Lance headed to the deck. A half-hour later, he spotted the man leaning over the rail. Morrison seemed to stare intently at the passing water.

Lance approached cautiously. "Evening."

Rigid lines appeared along Morrison's jaw and hand, but he didn't look up. "Good evening."

"Not thinking about jumping are you? Because that's a long way down." Lance turned with his back to the rail and crossed his arms. "Pardon me for saying so, but you don't look like you're enjoying the cruise. Is there anything I can do to help?"

"I'm here for my health. Not a good time. What are you, the cruise director?" The man turned dark eyes on him. "Not everyone hooks up with a pretty young woman. I've seen the way you watch her at mealtimes." He shrugged. "None of my business."

He was right. It wasn't any of his business. Lance waited for a disparaging remark and shoved his hands in his pockets to hide the clenched fists. He forced a smile to his face. "You're right. Molly is something else. Nothing like a shipboard romance, is there? Love 'em and leave 'em. No strings attached. Yep, that's the way I like it." God forgive him. He'd left the party days behind a long time ago and the words now left a sour taste in his mouth.

"So, you're just having a fling?"

"More or less." Would the guy buy his story? Lance hoped his game of toying with her affections would throw the man off the scent of them watching him. "So, why'd you come?"

"Just leaving behind some bad stuff."

"Clean ocean air is good for that."

Morrison pulled a cigarette from inside his jacket. His hand trembled as he lit it. "That's what I've heard."

Had they found any butts near the body in the warehouse? He'd have to make a call. Morrison smoked Marlboro Reds. He turned his attention to the horizon.

Streaks of magenta, lilac, and ginger, painted the sky. The sun's crimson sphere slowly began its descent beneath the waves. While Lance watched, the moon took the sun's place and instead of vibrant colors, the night was colored with shades of black and silver.

"Did you hear there's been a death on board? One of the crew members." He cut his gaze to Morrison. "Security suspects a murder."

Morrison's cigarette fell from his hands to the water below. "No, I hadn't heard. I guess with you seeing one of the crew members, you get the inside scoop." Perspiration glistened on the man's upper lip. "I thought crew and passengers weren't supposed to mix?"

"We were keeping things low key until she went on medical leave. We'll have to be more discreet when she resumes work." Lance pasted a goofy grin on his face.

Morrison turned to search his face. "You, sir, are not being truthful." He spun and marched down the deck until he disappeared around the bow.

The man had definitely been thrown. If he was an innocent bystander, Lance would eat his shoe. He smiled and strolled in the direction the man had taken. He'd keep his eyes open, ferret out some clues, then he'd send in the authorities.

He headed to his cabin for a time of rest and reflection. It'd been too long since he'd read his Bible, and he definitely needed some guidance. Not only in finding Antonio's killer, but in his relationship with Molly. Or lack thereof. What made him think he could love a woman who'd be at sea most of the year?

CYNTHIA HICKEY

8

Heavy pounding on the cabin door jarred Molly from her troubled sleep. She bolted upright, the thin sheet clutched to her chest. Her rapid breathing bounced off the walls, and her head spun from the sudden movement. Hilga cursed and rolled over, wrapping her pillow over her ears.

Outside the window, dawn broke. A thin beam of light lanced through the port and illuminated the room. Molly blinked and dragged her gaze back to the door. Whoever stood on the other side ceased the knocking. A faint scratching on the underside made Molly seize in panic. Suddenly, a white envelope slid through the quarter-inch space and skid to a halt. Like a snowy blot it stood out against the navy multi-purpose carpet.

Molly vacated the bed, wrapped the sheet around her, and shuffled toward the ominous rectangle. With shaking fingers, she lifted it from the floor, then opened the unaddressed message. Half a sheet of paper lay inside. Bold typed words screamed back at her.

Careful. You don't know what you're getting into.

Her blood chilled. No, she didn't. But through no fault of her own, she'd been drawn into one, possibly two murders. She wouldn't sit aside like a lamb led to slaughter and allow herself to become number three.

She scrambled into her red, white, and blue uniform, then dashed from the room, straight to the Plaza Deck and cabin 3106. A sleepy-eyed Lance answered her frantic knock.

"Molly? What is it?"

"I didn't know where else to go." She took a step back at the sight of him in only pajama bottoms. Her face heated, and she averted her gaze. "I'll wait here while you get dressed."

"I'll leave the door open." Lance grabbed a tee shirt and disappeared into the bathroom. Within seconds, he dragged Molly into his room.

A place filled with the fragrance of his aftershave. Her stomach flipped.

"This was shoved under my door." She handed him the warning.

A muscle in his jaw ticked as he read. His lips thinned. "This clarifies someone on this ship is a threat to you."

Molly's legs buckled. She swayed, and Lance lowered her onto a chair. "What do I do?"

He knelt in front of her. "Your job. Let me and the police do the rest. I'll keep you safe and they'll find out who is behind this."

She bent at the waist and let her hands dangle between her legs. "Lance, do you believe in God?"

"Yes." He tilted her chin until she looked at him. "Don't you?"

"I do, but…" Pulling away, Molly blinked against the tears welling in her eyes. "After my painful breakup, I prayed for a job that would take me away for a while. Photographer on a cruise ship seemed perfect. A direct answer from God. If I read him right. Why is this happening to me?"

Lance cupped her face and placed his lips against her forehead. The warm kiss and his tender touch broke the dam of tears she'd held at bay. He wiped them away with his thumbs. Molly's insides melted. That a man of Lance's size could be so tender, shocked her to her core. Her ex had been a smaller man with a mean streak the size of Texas. A spark of hope flickered in her heart.

"I don't know. Maybe you need strengthening. I'm new at this faith thing, Molly. I don't have all the answers. Why did I survive a shootout and my partner didn't? Out of all the cruises I could've taken, why am I on this one?" He straightened and shrugged. "Sometimes we don't get all the answers. We have to trust God to know what's best."

She glanced toward the open cabin door. Passengers strolled by in a steady, joyful stream. And here she sat, scared and broken, relishing a stranger's tender touch. Except Lance didn't feel like a stranger. She was more comfortable around him than she'd ever felt around Vince. "I need to get to work."

"The doctor excused you for a couple of days."

"It'll take my mind off things." She rose, laid a hand on his shoulder, and then moved to the door. Pausing, she glanced over her shoulder. "Thank you. I'll be at breakfast."

Lance frowned. "No, wait for me."

She nodded and stepped into the hall. Passengers glanced her way, and she forced a smile on her face. If Molly couldn't enjoy her cruise in paradise, she'd do her best to make sure others did.

Her faith was new too. Maybe she'd misunderstood

God's direction. She hadn't turned to him until after the brutal beating Vince had given her for breaking up with him. While she lay in a hospital bed, broken in more ways than one, a kindly nurse spoke the words that took root in her heart and sprouted into her soul. A life line. She grabbed hold, and hadn't let go of three words that held immense power. God loves you.

Now, her life was at risk again and she couldn't keep her mind off of a handsome police officer. She wasn't ready for romance. She merged with the passengers and allowed herself to be swept along.

Molly sniffed and composed herself before stepping into the clatter of breakfast aboard ship. Salt-cured bacon and the floury sweet smell of pancakes greeted her. The clatter of dishes and silverware serenaded those waiting in the buffet line. Hilga waved from her station, and the other photographer, Daniella, raised an eyebrow in question. Flashing them both a smile, Molly shrugged, then slid directly into her role as a happy picture taker. She'd rest later. Other than a raw spot on her neck and a slight headache, she suffered no other effects from yesterday. This morning's emotional wave ride was a towering tsunami threatening to crush her beneath its weight.

*

Lance entered the full dining room and inhaled deeply. Breakfast was his favorite meal of the day. Omelets, bacon, biscuits, and pancakes full of butter and maple syrup. He searched for Molly, spotted her snapping photos as she milled around the room, then he sauntered to the end of the buffet line. Grabbing a warm plate, he filled it with his favorite foods and moved to the nearest empty chair.

The ship would dock in Hilo by ten a.m. Before disembarking, he'd drop the note off with security then spend the day with a beautiful woman. And, he'd carry the camera this time. He wasn't about to take any more chances of someone knocking her down to steal it.

All his years on the force hadn't prepared him for a cruise ship murder. There weren't definite lines drawn of who headed up the investigation. Sure, security should have the responsibility, but somehow he lacked confidence in Jack Morley. The man didn't seem to be taking things as seriously as Lance thought he should.

He greeted his tablemates with a nod, then forked a healthy portion of pancake into his mouth. Maybe Morley was doing his best. After all, security people weren't trained to the same degree as detectives. He'd check with him after breakfast. See if he'd contacted the FBI.

Before sleeping last night, Lance had taken advantage of the free internet service and did some research. A lot of crimes at sea went unsolved. Mostly disappearances with the occasional death sprinkled in for variety. Often ruled a suicide. He vowed not to let it happen this time.

After eating his fill, he motioned for Molly to join him, and then headed down to the security office. She kept glancing over her shoulder.

"What are you looking for?"

"Morrison. I'm going to take as many pictures of him as possible. One of them has to match up to one of the profile photos."

Lance gripped her elbow. "Just don't make a nuisance of yourself. If he is our guy, you don't want to scare him off or anger him. You ought to leave it to security, or me. We're trained for this."

"He's hard to get a picture of. I tried the first day, and he covered his face." She stared up at him. "Doesn't that sound suspicious?"

He laughed. "A lot of people are camera shy."

"Just not you."

"Nope. I take good pictures. Bet you wouldn't guess I paid my way through college by doing some modeling." He clamped his mouth shut. Where did that come from? Did he just let that secret out of the bag?

She giggled. "That doesn't surprise me in the slightest. You have a very pretty face."

"Pretty?" Ouch! Women were pretty. Molly was pretty. Men, however, including himself, were not pretty.

The ship's security room door loomed before them. Lance knocked, waited for the call to enter, and ushered Molly in ahead of him.

Jack Morley looked up from a desk crammed into a corner of the small room. Two other desks lined the walls with bored men slumped in chairs behind them. Empty chairs, to seat visitors most likely, were stacked in a corner.

Morley straightened, tugging down his shirt. "Can I help you?"

Lance pulled the note from his pocket. "This was shoved beneath Molly's door this morning."

Waving them toward one of the empty chairs, Morley examined the note.

Lance offered it to Molly and perched on the corner of the SVP's desk.

Morley's eyes jerked up and he frowned. "Sounds threatening."

You think? Lance shook his head. "Have you contacted the FBI?"

"They don't have jurisdiction here."

"We're still in United States waters, aren't we?" Lance crossed his arms.

"Look, Mr. Spencer. Don't try to tell me how to do my job. We don't know that Antonio was murdered. No fingerprints, nothing." He rocked back in his chair. "Suicides happen all the time on the ship. Crew and staff work extremely hard and difficult hours. Some can't take the pressure. Antonio just broke up with his girlfriend. We found no evidence of foul play."

"I just came from a bad relationship," Molly said, "and I'm not trying to kill myself."

Morley shrugged. "Some people are stronger than others." His feet banged the floor as he righted his chair. "Look. I'll keep this in a file. You let us know if anything else happens. We're investigating and Hawaii PD is on the case. If someone else winds up dead, and it's clearly a murder, then I'll contact the FBI. Satisfied?"

Not really, but it was clear Lance didn't have a leg to stand on. So be it. He'd find the culprit and notify the FBI himself. "Thank you for your time." He pulled Molly to her feet and rushed her from the room.

"What did you make of that?" Her brows drew together.

"Not here. Wait until we get on deck." Lance practically dragged her topside. Once he'd found two empty deck chairs, they sat and he turned to face her.

"The man's incompetent, in my opinion. Not even on my worst day would I think a plastic bag over someone's face was a suicide."

"So, what do we do?"

"You continue snapping photos, and I'll investigate on my free time." Like when Molly was asleep.

"I want to help."

He shook his head. "Definitely not."

Red crept up from her collar and flooded her face. "Why not? It concerns me."

"Too dangerous."

"Oh, so now you're going to act like I'm the helpless little woman and you're the big bad He-man cop." She bolted to her feet and placed fists on her hips. "Well, I won't stand for it." The wind tossed her curls in riotous abandonment. Her eyes shot sparks of sapphire. She resembled a furious forest sprite.

"Settle down." He grinned. "Do you know how cute you are when you're mad?"

"Are you ... you can't be ..." She stomped her foot.

He laughed. "Okay, you can help. On my terms." Lord, don't let him regret his decision.

9

Molly stormed ahead of Lance down the gangplank to the waiting rental car. Again, a convertible. He definitely had good taste. She tossed Daniella, who leaned over the deck railing, a wave and clicked her seatbelt across her lap. The other photographer thought her crazy to take photos of the passengers during her time off, but Molly saw the investment. More photos taken, more bought, and more job security for herself.

Lance slid behind the wheel and flashed a dimple at her. "Don't be mad."

"I'm not." Why should she be mad at someone she barely knew? She blew a puff of air that stirred her bangs. Who was she kidding? His remarks left her feeling belittled and unworthy. Much like her childhood and prior engagement. Molly lifted her chin. "But I don't enjoy being ridiculed or talked down to."

"I'm sorry." He turned the key in the ignition. The car purred to life. "That wasn't my intention." He faced her. "Would you rather stay on the ship?"

"No. Hilo has a lot to see. We can explore this side of the island today and tomorrow we'll be docking on the other side." She slung a backpack over her shoulder and onto the back seat. "I don't want to miss a thing."

"Okay. The woman knows what she wants. Where to first?"

"Up the coast. I hope you wore comfortable shoes. There'll be a lot of walking."

"Don't worry about me." Lance stepped on the gas and they roared from the parking lot.

Molly stared at the ocean. She'd never grow tired of the beating surf, cry of seagulls, or vibrant emerald color surrounding her. Maybe she could reside on one of the islands during her time away from cruising. Someday, she'd meet a nice man, the right one, settle down, and a have a child or two. She glanced sideways at Lance.

The man was definitely worth looking at. Sculpted jaw, molded lips, thick wavy hair that her fingers itched to run through. Eyes the color of a deep dark sea at night. She sighed and glanced away. Trouble with a capital T.

A sign ahead caught her attention. Akaka Falls State Park. "Turn in there."

"What's to see?" Lance grimaced. "Not another high place is there?"

Molly grinned. "Waterfalls."

"Ought to be safe enough. It isn't like we're going over them in a boat, right? Or a cable? Tell me we'll be staying on our own two feet and not soaring through the air on a zip-line."

"Of course. Come on. It's a short uphill hike." Forgiving him for his earlier chauvinistic remarks, Molly grabbed his hand as soon as he exited the car. "You can carry the backpack. It has sandwiches and water bottles."

"I'd rather carry the camera."

"I don't think so." Molly adjusted it more securely around her neck. "No one is going to try and take it two days in a row. Yesterday was a random occurrence."

"You know that for a fact?" Lance retrieved the pack, then slipped his arms through the straps and shrugged it onto his shoulders.

"Close enough." She didn't know anything, but if she wanted Lance to let her help with the investigation, she'd have to be brave. Stay on top of things. Inside, she was a quivering mess. And it wasn't because of the gorgeous man beside her. Well, maybe a little bit.

A light drizzle started to fall, cooling the air. Glad she'd thought to bring a light jacket, Molly untied it from around her waist and pulled it on. A few tourists entered the path ahead of them, and they hesitated. "It'll be more enjoyable if it seems as if we're alone."

Lance's eyes warmed. "Sounds good to me."

Heat singed her cheeks. Could he turn any comment into a flirtatious one? Why couldn't she relax and enjoy his subtle suggestions? Would it be so bad to enjoy his company? Lots of people dabbled in harmless shipboard romances. Why couldn't she?

Because that's not how she lived her life. Especially her new one with a growing faith. Relationships were not to be trifled with. She'd have to be careful and keep Lance at arm's length.

"Let's go." She blazed the way down a path that cut through some of the thickest vegetation she'd ever seen. Small waterfalls broke up the denseness, filling the area with the singing of babbling brooks and splashing water. Vibrant foliage dotted the ground, and Molly continuously snapped pictures of hibiscus, white kukui blossoms, and pink cottage roses.

A roar greeted them as they turned the corner, and her eyes widened in anticipation.

Lance grabbed her arm. "What is that?"

"That, I believe, is Akaka Falls." She gripped his hand. "Hurry."

"Why? It isn't going anywhere." He dragged his feet, forcing Molly to tug on him.

They rounded a bend and broke through the trees. Her mouth dropped at the sight of the four hundred and twenty-foot waterfall crashing into a pool below them. The roar drowned out every sound around them. If she wanted to talk to Lance, she'd have to shout. Instead, she stepped to the overlook railing and lifted her face. The mist blowing off the fall kissed her cheeks, leaving droplets on her eyelashes. God's breath. Right there on the island of Hawaii. Her heart soared. She wiggled her fingers for Lance to join her.

When he didn't, she opened her eyes and glanced over her shoulder. He stood several feet away, plastered against the rock wall. His eyes bulged and he shook his head.

"Don't you want to see better?"

Color drained from his face. "No, I'm close enough, thank you."

*

Lance tried. He really had. He stepped up to the railing, caught one of the most magnificent views of his lifetime, then allowed his gaze to follow the waterfall's path to the pool beneath. A placid surface of water pounded by an unrelenting force pouring into it. Despite his throat seizing, he marveled at the beauty, then took three steps back, turning his attention instead on Molly as she soaked in her surroundings.

He'd experience the joy through her when they stood on high places. He stared at the hand she offered him.

"I'll hold your hand, Lance." Compassion filled her eyes. "I won't let go."

Everything inside him wanted to step next to her, entwine her small fingers with his, and soak in the moment. Instead, fear overwhelmed, squelching his desire, and he almost laughed at the thought of the petite woman holding him.

"Why are you afraid?"

There was no way he would tell her about the summer his tree house came crashing down. Or that his best friend had hit the ground, breaking both legs. Or that he'd hung from a branch for what seemed like forever until help arrived. The phobia would resolve itself. In time. Maybe. "Aren't you afraid of anything, Molly?"

Her arm fell to her side as her face paled. "I'm afraid of dying alone."

Words stuck in his throat. He wanted to make sure that didn't happen. He held out a hand, and she rushed to him. Folding his arms around her, he inhaled the fruity scent of the shampoo she'd used and the floral aroma from the flowers around them. His third day of knowing Molly Nicholson and she already owned a part of his heart. He was in deep trouble.

They continued on the path until voices carried to them on the tropical breeze and she pulled away. "I'm sorry. There's no reason to burden you with my feelings."

"My shoulders are big enough for anything you want to lay on them." He led her to a bench. "But God's are bigger."

"Listen who's talking, Mister afraid of heights." A sad smile teased at the corner of her mouth. "I'm learning He's in control, and struggling to believe it's true. My statement about being alone goes against what I've read in the Bible. I'm working on that too."

Tourists cluttered the trail, oohing and aahing over the majestic fall. Molly leaped to her feet and offered to take photos of the passengers she recognized. Squeals of joy echoed as a group of female high school graduates grouped in front of her and jostled for position.

Lance recognized the boisterous group from the ship. Their final fling before college.

When they'd finished and continued on their way, Molly resumed her seat next to Lance. She dug into the backpack, pulled out two sandwiches, handing him one along with a water bottle. "My mother raised me alone, working all hours. I spent most of my childhood entertaining myself. Then, when I got older, I moved from one failed romantic relationship to another. Looking for a love that would last a lifetime."

He could relate. Keeping his distance from women other than his partner left Lance feeling empty. For a while, he'd entered a life of bachelorhood. Like the apostle Paul. But, he'd come to his senses. He wasn't meant to spend his life without a woman by his side.

She glanced up with shimmering eyes. "I found that in Jesus, but it's still difficult to leave behind years of searching." She gave a nervous laugh. "I don't know why I'm telling you this."

"I'm honored that you have." He reclined against the back of the bench and gazed at the waterfall. It truly was a beautiful sight. He stared at the view while they ate.

"Come on." He stood and helped her to his feet. "I'd like to face a giant."

Her face lit up. "Really?"

"With you holding my hand." He winked and laughed as her cheeks flushed.

Together they stood against the rail of the lookout, Lance's heart in his throat the entire time. The earth didn't disappear from beneath his feet. He didn't fall to his death. Instead, he choked back his fear and placed an arm around the beautiful woman at his side.

10

L ance's body trembled as Molly leaned into him, alerting her to the fact heights affected him more than she'd thought. Poor guy.

She ducked out from under his arm and grabbed his hand. "Come on, hero. Let's find a place that serves coffee. I think you need it more than I do."

"That's an understatement."

They finished the hike trail loop, seeing local fauna and more waterfalls, none of which matched the majesty of Akaka. Lance relaxed beside her, his fingers warming in her hand. She'd thought about parasailing on Maui. Wondered whether she'd be brave enough. Obviously that was out of the question. Unless she went alone. And she didn't see that happening. There was no way she'd subject Lance to the horror of sailing above a speck of a boat. Somehow, she knew, despite his fear, he'd do it if she insisted.

"Let's park somewhere in Hilo and stroll the streets and soak up some of the local culture."

Lance held the car door open for her. "Thank you."

"For letting you be a gentleman?" Molly grinned.

"Yes, and more." He loped to the driver's side and vaulted over the door and into his seat like a stunt man.

What a contrast. Movie star handsome with alpha

male tendencies that she found irresistible, and a debilitating phobia.

The drive back to Hilo was silent except for the song of pounding surf and wind. Occasionally Molly tore her gaze away from the ocean's beauty and studied Lance's profile. He appeared deep in thought, eyes straight ahead, the breeze blowing his gorgeous head of hair. She wanted to ask what he was thinking, but didn't want to disturb the comfortable silence between them.

In the past, she'd always felt the need to talk. To fill the air between her and someone else with words. Sitting beside Lance didn't require speech, and there were no words to describe the electricity between the two of them except shocking. What was she going to do when the cruise ended? There'd be a void in her life she doubted another man could fill.

"How about here?" Lance pulled the convertible into a parking space facing Hilo Bay. Surfers and windsurfers dotted the sea with splashes of color.

"Perfect." She forced herself to wait until he came around to help her out. She could get used to being treated like a lady. Good manners, being valued for being a woman, instead of looked down upon for being weaker, all were things she'd been seeking whether she'd known it or not.

She linked her arm through Lance's and allowed him to lead the way down the sidewalk. Pots of blooming flowers filled the air with their heady perfume and mingled with the scents of baked goods, coffee, and chocolate.

They stopped in front of a window displaying chocolate crèmes. Molly's mouth watered. In the window glass, she caught the reflection of a man in khaki shorts and a flowered Hawaiian shirt. A normal sight on the islands, except for the fact that the clothes looked new, still wearing their creases, and his attention seemed to be focused on her and Lance. She shook off the thought. Paranoid, that's what she was.

"Look." She pointed to a white-fronted store. "An outdoor coffee shop. We can watch the water while we drink." She tugged Lance along.

Robert Morrison was seated at one of the wrought-iron tables. Perfect. She chose the table next to him and turned her back. No need to scare him away. But if someone joined him, she'd be able to hear their conversation.

Lance scowled and chose the seat facing the other table. He leaned close to her. "Not very subtle."

Molly shrugged. "I would like a tall, frozen mocha coffee. No whipped cream. If they don't have that, could you order the closest thing to it?" If he wanted to be the alpha male, she'd let him pick up the tab.

"Your wish is my command." He raised a hand until a young girl approached, and placed their orders.

Across the street, the stranger appeared to window-shop. Considering Molly could see not only her reflection from where she sat, but the other man's, she suspected he spied on them. "Lance."

"Uh-hmm."

"That man seems to be following us."

He turned to where she motioned. "Really? Why do you think so? There are crowds of people filling the street."

"He's everywhere we are." When had Lance's cop instinct disappeared? Shouldn't the hair on the back of his neck be prickling? She knew, in her gut, that the man was overly interested in them.

Their order arrived and she took a big gulp of the icy drink, squinting against the rush of frozen pain to her throat. "What time is it?"

"One o'clock."

"I have to be back at the ship by two. I guess we'll know if he's following us if he shows up there." She pinched the bridge of her nose.

"Don't look, but Morrison is leaving."

Molly turned. The man set off at a brisk pace toward the harbor.

"I told you not to look!"

"Sorry." She shrugged. "Where's he going?"

"Across the street. The mystery man is now strolling in the same direction."

"Do you think they know each other?"

Lance raised an eyebrow. "Do you want to follow?"

She bolted to her feet, knocking over her chair. "I'd love to." How exciting! They'd get to be spies. What could happen in broad daylight, surrounded by people, with Lance beside her? There had been the camera incident, but that'd been nothing but an attempted mugging, or a ploy to frighten her. She was certain.

Lance grabbed her arm and pulled her back when she turned to run. "Slow down, speedy. We'll move along, window shopping. Totally engrossed in each other. That way they don't suspect a thing." He winked. "This is my favorite part of under-cover work."

"Done a lot of it, have you?"

He grinned, slung an arm around her shoulder, and pulled her close. Solid, warm, smelling better than the rarest orchids of Hawaii. All apt descriptions for Lance Spencer.

Oh, man. She was a goner.

*

He ought to be ashamed of himself, but Lance would use even the act of spying to keep Molly close. She hugged his arm and kept up a continuous chatter, even occasionally laying her head against his arm. Three days ago he would've punched anyone who told him he'd fall for a curly haired woman who barely reached his shoulder.

The more they walked, the more convinced he was that the colorfully dressed man followed Morrison. And Morrison knew it. They seemed to be searching for a safe place to meet. When the two ducked into an art gallery, Lance leaned with his back against the outside wall and pulled Molly into an embrace.

She gave a sharp intake of breath that threatened to steal his away. Then, her lips spread in an impish grin. "I like this stakeout thing."

From the corner of his eye, he spotted Morrison and the other man exiting the gallery. Morrison now held a large envelope.

Lance lowered his head and kissed Molly, turning her so that her back was flush against the wall. Hopefully, Morrison wouldn't recognize them. The world spun in a kaleidoscope of brilliant color and clarity. He pulled her closer and deepened the kiss. Time ceased to exist. For a moment, he forgot why they were there. Their surroundings settled back into place when he lifted his head and gazed into eyes deeper than the Pacific Ocean.

He caught a glimpse of the back of the two men's heads as they strolled away and remembered what he'd been doing. "Sorry. They were coming out."

Molly blinked. "No problem. Part of the cover." She looked away. Her cheeks flushed crimson. "It's obvious they know each other. Oh, no! I'm going to be late for work again." With the speed of a gazelle she bounded to the car.

Lance dashed after her. He didn't think the goofy grin on his face would go away anytime soon.

They roared down the road. The *Destiny* rose majestic and white above the sea. Molly's feet pounded up the gangplank. They burst inside and Lance caught a glimpse of the clock in the Grand Foyer. One fifty-five. She'd made it. With a quick flash of teeth, Molly tossed him a wave and headed toward the service elevator.

He laughed and shook his head. Not so fast, missy. He sprinted for the stairs. When he reached the bottom, chest heaving, a crick in his side, shoulder throbbing, Molly stood at the bottom giggling.

"I knew I couldn't get away from you. I'm assigned to take photos of the onboard activities today."

Lance struggled to breathe. "I'll tag along, thank you." And later that evening, he'd ponder the feelings behind their kiss. It might have been given on the spur of the moment, but he wouldn't forget it for a long time. His insides still danced the jitterbug.

Their first stop was aerobics class. Lance remained in the hall, occasionally glancing through the window, itching to move on to something more interesting. Then they moved to skeet shooting. His nerves stayed on edge with each bang of the rifle.

Laughter and good-natured ribbing rang with each shot. Made him wish he wasn't injured so he could shoulder a rifle. He'd sit and watch others enjoy the sunny afternoon, while keeping an eye on Molly. He turned to choose a lounge chair and came face-to-face with Hawaiian Shirt.

11

Are you Lance Spencer with the LA police department?" The man stared impassively at Lance, not removing the dark sunglasses that covered his eyes. One hand hidden in the pocket of his shorts.

Lance put a hand to his back to make sure his shirt hung far enough to hide the weapon tucked in the waistband of his pants. "Yes."

Mister Hawaiian Shirt jerked his head to the other side of the deck. Lance followed him a few feet away from the shooters; every nerve tingled on alert. Glancing at Molly while she continued snapping pictures, Lance asked, "Who are you?"

The man pulled a badge from his pocket. "Agent Will Cohn with the FBI. I'm working undercover on suspicion of embezzlement with Robert Morrison. Do you have a license to carry on board that weapon of yours?"

"Yes. I wouldn't have gotten on the ship with it if I didn't." Lance studied the identification then handed it back. "Why are you telling me this and how did you know who I was?"

"I'm aware that you and Miss Nicholson spotted me

today." His mouth quirked. "Fantastic way of trying to look unobtrusive, by the way. What a kiss. Anyway, I don't want you coming after me and blowing my cover. As for knowing who you are, let's say the bureau has sources."

Lance ignored the man's comment about his behavior with Molly. He didn't want anything to sully the memory of her lips on his. "What did you give Morrison in the store?"

"Good eye. I misled him with some financial matters. The man's a shark. He'll bite anything that smells like easy money." With his index finger, Cohn pushed his glasses farther on his nose. "He thinks I'm playing both sides of the fence, so to speak. Grease my palm, and I'll do the same for you."

Lance nodded, "Are you aware of the murder in Honolulu and the one on board?"

"Yes, but the Honolulu PD hasn't asked for the FBI's help on this. Yet. I'm now a passenger on board the *Destiny*. Keep your eyes open and let me know if you see something that warrants my attention. Otherwise, we're just two passengers onboard the same ship. See you around." Cohn marched across the deck and out of sight.

Molly had stopped taking pictures and stared at him. Should he tell her who the man really was or let her think they'd struck up a random conversation? Considering her willingness to shadow Morrison, being upfront seemed like the best approach.

"I'll tell you later." Lance called before lowering himself onto a deck chair. He felt better knowing the FBI was onboard. Sure, they weren't focusing on the murders, but he'd have backup if needed. Once he found the killer, he could turn him over to Cohn and enjoy the rest of his vacation. With Molly at his side.

The sun began to set over the horizon, showing off its brilliance in painted strokes of magenta and purple. Lance eased his arm from the sling, leaned back, and let the view restore both his body and soul. If he hadn't gone to church as a boy, seen God's redemption as an adult, the beauty of nature alone would have convinced him of God's presence.

His gaze followed Molly as she snapped a picture of a couple posed against the railing, the sun's crimson face in the background. What would happen to him and Molly at the end of the cruise? Did he really want to pursue a long distance relationship, or any relationship for that matter? He'd been shot once. Chances are the next time could be fatal. Would Molly be willing to take the risk of being left a police widow?

Good grief. They'd known each other three days and he was thinking marriage? He'd lost it. Definitely. Besides, Molly made it clear she wasn't looking for a love interest.

*

Lance's gaze burned a hole in Molly's back and set her skin on fire, her nerves on high alert knowing he watched every move she made. She stole a peek at him. To the casual observer, he'd be nothing more than a passenger at complete and total relaxation. Enjoying the sunset. She knew different. If anything appeared remotely dangerous, he'd spring from the lounge chair like a leopard pouncing on its prey.

Curiosity about the man in the Hawaiian shirt nagged at her. She'd seen the butt of Lance's weapon when he'd reached for it. The thought of him carrying a gun sent ice through her veins. Then, he'd relaxed. Who was the man?

"Put your arm around her. Step back. Smile. Perfect." She snapped the newlyweds with the colorful evening sky behind them. Ah, love. Was it in God's plan for her to experience the overwhelming, fiery passion of a man not only in love with her but with God? Well, a girl could dream. And pray. For the next eight months, she had a job to do. No time for her head to be in the clouds. Love would have to come later. If it ever chose to show its elusive face at all.

She motioned for Lance to follow, then led the way to the Martini Bar. Glass tables sparkled beside white leather chairs. A blue light lit up the bar from underneath, giving the room an underwater feel. Elongated lighting gave the impression of iridescent jellyfish. Muted voices rose above the piano music. A classy place for well-dressed passengers. Definitely different from the dark and smoky crew bar below deck. She'd sat there once to visit with Hilga, and spent the next few hours smelling like an ashtray. No thank you.

Lance chose a seat alone at a far table. Molly circulated and took photos of smiling people with glasses raised as they made toasts she couldn't hear. Either the captain and SVP had managed to keep Antonio's death a secret, or the passengers chalked it up to an experience at sea. No one seemed afraid or apprehensive. Maybe their attitude was the right one. Life went on. Could she treat Antonio's demise as a random occurrence and not fret about it?

She'd let Lance continue to play the role as her shadow, but she'd enjoy the dream job she'd taken and stop fearing that danger lurked around every corner. Her hand stilled in taking pictures when Hawaiian shirt entered, dressed in white pants and a black linen shirt. She focused the camera lens and snapped a photo.

"Put the camera down, Molly." Lance whispered in her ear. Placing his hand over hers, he lowered the Nikon.

"But he could be a suspect."

"He's not. I said I'll tell you later. Trust me."

She turned and studied his face. He smiled. The dimple she loved so much winked from his cheek. Traces of five o'clock shadow outlined his jaw. "Okay, but—"

He laid a finger on her lips. "No buts." Before she could react, he'd stepped back and resumed his seat.

Fine. She'd tell her thoughts to the One who always listened. God never shushed His children. He'd understand her worries about Morrison and Hawaiian shirt. With her nose in the air, she marched across the room to where several honeymoon couples snuggled and offered to take photos.

Thirty minutes later, she approached the table where Lance sipped a cola. "Do we talk here, or somewhere more private?"

"This is really eating you up, isn't it?" He grinned, downed the last of his soda, and then stood. "How about a stroll around the Promenade deck?"

Her feet ached, but she'd keep the news to herself if that's what it took to find out the identity of the mystery man. Lance's secret had been kept long enough. If he didn't spill the beans within the next five minutes, she'd shove him overboard.

He laughed as if he could read her mind. "Relax."

With his hand on the small of her back, he guided her from the bar and up a level.

Stars littered the sky like diamonds against a navy background. Waves sloshed against the bow of the ship. The romance of the setting wasn't lost on Molly. She sighed.

Lance entwined his fingers with hers and slowly swayed their hands as they walked. "The man you're so keen on is FBI agent Will Cohn."

"FBI! Finally."

"He's following Morrison, not because of the deaths, but because he suspects him of embezzling."

"Oh." That meant she and Lance were still on their own. She sagged into the nearest chair. She'd wanted to be brave. Keep her chin up and move forward. She failed miserably. Instead, she wanted to curl into a ball and cry.

Lance sat beside her and pulled her into his arms. Molly rested her head against his broad solid chest. "It'll be okay. Don't you trust me?" He tilted her chin so she'd look at him.

"Yes." She searched his face, highlighted by the moon's silver glow. "But you're one man."

"With a big God. I'm good at my job, Molly. I'm committed to protecting you first, and searching for a killer second." His good arm tightened around her. She closed her eyes, wishing for a moment he held her as a man holds the woman he loves.

"You were shot once, Lance." Her heart constricted. "What if it happens again?"

She didn't think she could stand the thought. When he'd told her the FBI was onboard, her fear had evaporated, only to come crashing back with the force of a tidal wave when he'd said the agent watched Morrison for something other than murder. When would the authorities take Antonio's death seriously?

After someone else died?

12

Molly unlocked her cabin door. "Good night, Lance."

"Good night."

She watched him walk through the cracked door until it clicked shut. Bolting the lock, she moved to the edge of her bed where she waited, contemplating the danger of roaming the ship alone. Some of the passengers would stay out late in the casino and the bar. The sparse night crew would be working. But was it enough?

Morrison killed Antonio. She knew it. Could she bet her life on it? There lingered the real question.

Where was Hilga? Molly glanced at the clock. Almost midnight. Her roommate had duty at six-thirty in the morning. Reckless woman. Molly flopped back on the bed. Who was she to judge? If she didn't get any sleep, she'd be a zombie by lunchtime and no good to anyone.

She forced herself out of bed and shuffled into the bathroom. After changing into her nightgown and robe, she washed off her makeup. The face reflected in the mirror flickered a glimmer of her old self. Back to a time when loneliness had no hold on her and the promise of love brightened her future. The image staring back appeared way too serious. Yes, a glimmer showed in her eyes. Possibly the result of time spent with Lance. Should she dare hope?

There'd been absolutely no reason for Vince Nelson to spend time with another woman. He'd showered Molly with gifts and empty phrases of love. Spouting about her beauty, when all he'd wanted to do was own her and still play the field.

Molly slapped the faucet handle to hot. Was saving yourself for marriage such a bad thing? Couldn't he have waited a few more months? She splashed water on her face and filled her hand with a moisturizing cleanser. The beating he had given her after she broke it off left her feeling like the doormat he'd always wanted. Later, she'd realized God's hand in the dissolution of her relationship. She thanked him every day.

What if she did get together with Lance? Would he turn out the same? Most likely. A detective who'd seen the gritty side of life. It had to harden a person. But then there was his faith to soften him.

Molly washed her face with circular movements. Maybe Lance was the one who …

A knock on the door reverberated. Her eyes snapped open. The cleanser seeped under her eyelids and stung her eyes. Quickly she scooped water in her hands to rinse it away.

"Molly! Open the door. Please." Hilga's frantic voice cut through the wall. Molly grabbed a towel to scrub away the remnants of soap and water.

Her roommate whimpered. "Please, let me in."

Molly's fingers fought with the lock. Her breathing matched Hilga's harsh gasps. Once she swung the door wide, Hilga tripped inside. Molly slammed it shut, sliding the deadbolt into place.

Hilga thrust an envelope at her. "This was given to me when my shift ended. Some kid ran up and shoved it in my hand. What are you mixed up in?" She shakily sat on her bunk.

"What's in it?" Molly's hands trembled.

"Open it and see. If you dare. Almost scared me to death." Hilga laid on her bunk, her forearm resting on her forehead. "That's what I get for opening somebody else's mail."

"Maybe you'll learn." Molly fumbled with the envelope and pulled out a single sheet of white printer paper. The words: *Keep your nose where it belongs and no more pictures* jumped out at her. Her heart threatened to stop with the next line. *Or be prepared to meet the fate of your friend.*

"Who gave this to you?" She fell on the bunk beside Hilga. Was the note about Antonio, or someone who hadn't been murdered yet?

"Some kid with long hair, expensive jeans with holes in the knees, and gauges in his ears." Hilga peered from beneath her arm. "This isn't about Antonio, is it?"

"Half the teenage boys on this ship fit that description." Molly sighed. "Would you recognize him if you saw him again?"

Hilga bolted to a sitting position. "You aren't thinking about looking for this kid, are you? It's midnight!"

"He might be in the arcade. Kids hang out there until all hours. Let's go."

"You're insane. At least let me get a man to go with us."

Molly shook her head. "There's no time. The boy

will disappear." She slipped on a pair of shorts under the oversized tee shirt she'd donned, then grabbed Hilga's hand. "Please."

"Fine." She swung her legs over the edge of the bed. "I'm as stupid as you. If I wind up dead, I'm coming back to haunt you."

*

Lance sat in a dark corner of the bar and watched Morrison take a seat at the counter. The man ordered a beer, then swung around on his stool to study the other passengers. Lance lifted his glass of water, with a slice of lemon, and peered over the rim. He'd ordered his drink in a martini glass in order to fit in. Would Morrison fall for the deception?

When the man glanced his way and narrowed his eyes, Lance lifted his glass in welcome. Morrison nodded, then swiveled back around when his beer arrived. He immediately chugged it, slapped the bottle on the bar, and then ordered another one. He stared into the amber liquid of his second drink like a man who pondered the world's problems.

FBI agent Cohn entered and took a seat at the opposite end of the polished counter, not acknowledging Morrison. His gaze flicked to Lance, then away.

Content to sit back and watch the drama unfold in front of him, Lance leaned against the booth's back and crossed his legs. He sat up when he spotted Molly and her roommate quick-walk past the door. What was she up to now?

Morrison slid from his stool.

Lance stood and followed the man from the bar, taking care not to be seen. Morrison snuck from the corner to a potted plant, then to the open door, clearly following the two women.

Molly and her companion stepped into the elevator. "Not that one, Hilga," Molly said. "We need the Promenade deck."

Announce your destination to the world, Molly. Well, at least he knew where they headed. What was she thinking? He'd told her not to go anywhere alone. Another woman didn't count. Not in Lance's opinion, anyway. He wasn't sure what he'd do with her when he got his hands on her, but it wouldn't be pleasant.

He sprinted for the stairs and raced down six levels, sliding through the door as Molly and Hilga headed down the hallway. Morrison was nowhere to be seen. The two women disappeared into the bright, loud arcade. Lance slipped behind a game booth where he could hear without being seen.

"Do you see him, Hilga?" Molly clasped an envelope to her chest.

"Do you see how many kids are in here?" Hilga crossed her arms. "Doesn't anyone sleep anymore? Wait. I think that's him."

Molly dashed forward and grabbed the arm of a kid playing a game where his character shot aliens. Lance moved closer.

"Do you recognize this?" Molly waved the envelope in his face.

Without breaking stride, the boy glanced at her, then shrugged. "Maybe."

"Who gave it to you?"

"You want information, it'll cost you, lady."

Molly stiffened. "You watch too much television. I'm a crewmember on board this ship, and I demand you answer me."

The boy sighed and turned to face her. "You're one of the photographers. I recognize you, so actually, you aren't a crew member, you're a concessionaire. You have a contract."

Lance bit his lip to keep from laughing as Molly's mouth fell open.

"How do you know this?"

"I'm a genius, what do you think? I read up on the cruise before we set sail. The brochure they mail out is as thick as a book. There's nothing else to do on a plane." His shoulders slumped.

"I was in here about an hour ago, totally engrossed in my game. Almost won, too, until some dude in a baseball cap tossed the envelope in front of me, slapped down a twenty-dollar bill, and told me to give it to her." He pointed at Hilga. "That's all I know." He held up a hand. "Before you ask, I wouldn't recognize him if I saw him. I never turned around. Just pocketed the cash. Can I go now?"

Molly nodded.

The boy shuffled past Lance, caught a glimpse of him, skittered to the side like a rabbit who spotted a predator, then quickened his pace. Lance smiled.

"That was a waste of time." Hilga stomped her foot. "I could've been sleeping."

"You were too afraid to sleep." Molly frowned. "You shouldn't have read this. Now, the killer might think you know something."

"What are you talking about?" Hilga's shriek rose above the music and jangle of the arcade games.

The killer? What did she hold in that envelope? If it was something bad enough to frighten them, then it was double certain the two women shouldn't be roaming the ship when most of the crew and passengers were sleeping.

Lance stepped from his hiding place. "Molly, what have I said about roaming the ship without me?"

13

Molly shrieked and plastered her back against the wall. Her stomach lurched like the ship was plummeting to the bottom of the ocean. "We, uh, well …" He might as well know the truth; if he didn't already. She thrust the envelope at him. "I wanted to find out where this came from."

A disappointed frown marred Lance's features. Guilt twinged in her chest. Maybe searching without him was stupid, but she had Hilga with her. The woman was an Amazon! Almost as tall as his six feet. If she wasn't such a scaredy-cat, Molly would be perfectly safe with her. No one would attack two people, would they?

The tic in Lance's jaw jumped at the speed of a racehorse. His brows drew together as he read, and he huffed through his nose. At any moment, Molly expected steam to shoot from his red-tipped ears.

Shoving aside the flutters in her stomach, she crossed her arms and waited for his lecture. Hilga tried to squeeze past her. Molly planted herself in her roommate's way. "Stay," she hissed. "You're part of this now."

"You can go," Lance said, his gaze still on the paper in his hand.

Hilga shot Molly an apologetic look, then sprinted for the elevator. Traitor! Molly sucked in a deep breath and focused on Lance. Amazing how brown eyes could suddenly become cold and hard.

"Do you need to see the doctor?" He stared impassively at her.

Molly licked her lips. "What?"

"Is your finger broken?"

"No, why?"

"I thought maybe it was since you chose not to call me before setting out on your own to hunt down the author of a threatening letter. I've given you my cell phone number." He held up a hand to stop her protests. "Your roommate doesn't count." After inserting the note back in the envelope, he tucked it in his pocket, then grabbed Molly's arm.

"I'll escort you back to your room and pick you up at six." He leaned closer. "Are you aware that Morrison followed you and Hilga as far as the elevator?"

Molly swallowed against the mountain-size lump in her throat.

"If you'd been alone, I have no doubts that one or both of you would've disappeared."

"So, you do think Morrison's the killer!"

"I never said I thought otherwise. Only that we need to keep our options open." Lance pressed the button for the elevator. "What you did was stupid. Empty-headed!"

Molly entered first. When Lance stepped in, the temperature dropped twenty degrees. His rigid stance worried a hole in her stomach. She clutched her arms around her midsection and shivered. Was he taking her to her room to hit her? His last statement echoed

Vince's vocabulary verbatim. She didn't know what kind of a guy Lance was. What he was capable of doing. Fear clawed at her chest. Her leg muscles bunched. She needed to get out of there.

The elevator pinged to a stop. When the doors began to slide open, she sent a sharp jab to Lance's gut with her elbow. With a grunt, he bent over. She shot forward, escaping through the slight gap in the doors. As she dashed out she toppled a large trash can to block Lance's way. The echo of something hitting the wall made her flinch.

"Molly!"

The anger in his voice spurred her faster. Experience with Vince told her she needed to get away. Now. Past the casino and bar, through the arcade, around empty restaurant tables, until she burst through the women's restroom door.

Her chest heaved, her stomach roiled, and her body trembled. She closed her eyes and leaned against the wall. *Help me, God.* She'd been stupid to trust a man so soon after Vince. Especially one in a career riddled with violence. A victim himself of an act that left his partner dead. Maybe some of the world's evil rubbed off on him. And she was stuck on a ship with him for twelve nights.

Was she completely wrong? Could Lance be a nice guy trying to control his temper after she'd disobeyed a direct order?

Tears poured down her face. The forceful beat of her heart hurt her chest. Who was he to tell her what to do? They'd known each other all of four days. She hadn't gone alone, after all.

She banged her head on the wall behind her. Stupid,

stupid, stupid.

Footsteps pounded outside the restroom, then paused. Molly held her breath. The door swung open.

*

The fear-stricken look on Molly's face when he barged into the restroom almost ripped Lance's heart from his chest. "Molly?"

She sniffled and slid along the wall away from him, avoiding his gaze. "Go away."

"What's wrong?" God, what could he do? She was afraid of him. Ridiculous. Lance would rather cut off his arm, then lay a hand on her. "Molly, look at me." He stood in front of her.

She raised red-rimmed eyes to his. Though she trembled, she met his gaze. "If you're going to hit me, get it over with."

"What?" He staggered back. "Why would I do that?" He knelt in front of her and took her hands in his. "I would never hurt you."

She sniffed. "The anger rolled off you in waves, Lance. I could feel it."

"Sure, you made me mad running off like that, but I wouldn't hit you." He smiled. "Maybe lock you in your room." What monster did this to her? He'd like to wrap his hands around the man's neck.

She returned a slight resemblance of a smile. "I'm sorry. I should've realized you weren't the type. Living on pins and needles the way I have the last couple of days has screwed up my thinking."

Lance cupped her face. "Sweetheart, the only thing you have to apologize for is taking off without telling me." He stood. "If I had been the bad guy, I'd expect you to run, but fight if you have to. With all you have.

You've got a sharp elbow. I could teach you some more self-defense moves. Would you like that?"

Her face brightened, and she wiped her tears away with her sleeve. "Very much."

"We'll practice tomorrow. At the beach. I'll teach you how to throw me over your shoulder." It would hurt like the dickens, especially with his wound not completely healed, but he'd do anything to put a smile back on her face.

Lance slid to the floor, pulling Molly with him. The cold tile bit into his bottom and lower back, seeping into his wounded shoulder. He shifted position to relieve the pressure of his gun digging into his spine. "You were wise to run when you saw signs of my anger." God, help him do this without scaring her off. "I told you about my partner being killed."

Molly nodded.

"I was more angry that day than I'd ever been. The husband had beaten his wife into a coma. I didn't only talk Abby into making one more call, I badgered her into it out of rage. I wanted the man to pay for what he'd done. And I wanted to be the one to serve the justice.

"He fired a gunshot out his front door, striking Abby in the chest." His throat tightened. "I had no idea she'd already changed out of her Kevlar vest. I couldn't see straight enough to put mine on. His next shot caught me in the shoulder. I emptied my weapon into him." All because of a red-hot rage boiling in his gut. Two people had been killed.

Molly stared into his face. "I know you're carrying, but are you trying to tell me I need to worry about you shooting me?"

Lance laughed through his tortured throat. "No, I'm trying to tell you that I struggle with anger issues. Always have. God's dealing with me, but I'm a work in process."

"We all are. I'm impulsive, in case you haven't noticed." She bumped him with her shoulder. "You could've just told me that you deal with anger. But, thank you, for sharing what is obviously a painful part of your life."

"You're welcome." He pulled her close for a quick hug. "Let's get you back to your room."

"I really am sorry, Lance." Tears welled in her eyes again. "You've given me no reason to respond the way I did."

"Do you want to talk about it?"

Did she? Did his kind words mean she could trust him? Vince had been full of sugar too. Once upon a time. *Help me out, Lord.* "Sure."

He held the door for her, and matched his longer stride to hers. "Your ex hit you?" Or worse. A fist gripped his heart.

"That's an understatement." She took a deep breath. "Vince wasn't content to wait for something I wasn't ready to give." With a trembling hand, she tucked her hair behind one ear. "I broke up with him. He beat me bad enough to put me in the hospital. His "other" girlfriend visited me there. He'd been playing the same game with her."

Lance's blood boiled. Heat rose in his face and he fought the urge to clench his fists. "Where is he now?"

A glimmer of a smile crossed her lips. "In jail. For another year. We both pressed charges. Considering the scratches down his face matched the skin under my fingernails, it wasn't a hard case to win."

"Good for you." He wanted to hug her. Despite her quick attempt to flee what she thought to be a volatile situation, Molly showed spunk. She'd pull through in a tough spot. He had no doubt, if the situation warranted, the claws would come out and she'd fight like a cornered tiger.

"Did Vince, uh, …" Why was it so hard? He'd asked the question a hundred times to other traumatized women. "Use force?"

Molly's face hardened. "This conversation is finished."

Okay. Question answered.

The empty corridor leading to her cabin taunted him with an unnatural silence. Fans from the air conditioner whirred from behind metal vents. He pulled Molly closer to him and withdrew his weapon from the waistband of his pants. The quiet could be from everyone sleeping since it was one a.m., but every nerve snapped with energy. His cop sense worked overtime. "If something happens, stay behind me."

She made a strangled sound and gripped his arm. Her nails bit into his skin. "What if it's Hilga? What if he got her? What if—"

"Don't jump to conclusions, Molly." He paused in front of her cabin. "Can I have the key?"

She handed it to him and plastered herself to the wall. After unlocking the door, Lance pushed it open with his foot.

Hilga's bed was still made. The bathroom door hung open. "Your roommate isn't here."

CYNTHIA HICKEY

14

Molly peered under Lance's arm. *God, please, not Hilga.* She said she was going back to the room. What if the killer got her? She gripped the back of Lance's shirt with sweaty hands. "We need to find her."

"Calm down." He removed her hands and pulled her into the room, closing the door behind them. "Where's her boyfriend's cabin?"

"I don't know his name." Molly collapsed on the nearest bed. She should've asked the guy's name. What kind of a friend was she? She ran her hands through her hair. "She could be lying somewhere right this minute with a bag over her face."

"We don't know that." Lance strode into the bathroom and whipped aside the shower curtain.

The rattle of the rings on the metal pole grated over Molly's nerves. He left the bathroom and moved to the lone closet.

Fatigue settled on her shoulders like a wave of sea water. She struggled to breathe. Fought to rise through the churning surface of fear.

She had to be at breakfast at six o'clock. She wouldn't make it. At this point, if the purser wanted to fire her, she'd gladly accept, pack her bags, and fly home when they docked at eight a.m.

Lance closed the closet. "You need to get some sleep."

She bolted to her feet. "I'm not staying here by myself!" Her heart battered the walls of her ribs. He couldn't leave her alone like this. How could she sleep? Hilga was missing and Morrison was after her. "You can sleep here. Hilga's bunk is empty."

"You know I can't stay with you. Not only is it improper, but a crew member and a passenger together is a big no-no." He laid his hands on her shoulders and massaged them. His eyes locked onto hers. "I know you're scared, Molly, but I'll pick you up in the morning. Don't leave without me. Lock the doors. Don't open for anyone but me, and you'll be fine. I'll alert security that Hilga isn't in her room. We'll find her." He planted a kiss on her forehead and left.

Molly slid the deadbolt and collapsed on the bed without removing her clothes. Her forehead tingled where his lips touched her. What a ninny. There was a murderer on board and all she could think about was a kiss? And a peck on the forehead at that. If she wanted to dwell on kissing, the knee-knocking one onshore should've filled her thoughts.

She shook her head. When the danger ended, she'd have plenty of time to focus on her feelings for the protective and handsome cop.

What had she gotten involved in? How did one little picture cause so much turmoil? No one could make out the guy's face. By the picture's standard, it took a stretch of the imagination to determine whether a murder even happened. Yet, it had. The police confirmed the death. Had Antonio not been killed, she might have left things alone. Spent the week doing her job, instead of fearing for her life. She didn't know the identity of the killer. Why couldn't he leave her alone?

She'd shown a moment of weakness in the elevator and the restroom. Well, no more. She pounded the mattress. There'd be no lying down and waiting to be killed. Not for her. With Lance's help, she'd find out who stalked her and have the guy put away. No more cowering. If cornered, she'd fight. Better to go down in a fight, than a weak victim.

She'd pressure the police to step up their investigation. Badger the FBI into looking at Morrison as a murder suspect. If he proved innocent, she'd nag them into looking elsewhere. And in the meantime, she'd find Hilga. Maybe the note had sent her friend into hiding below deck. Or in her boyfriend's cabin. She could've made him promise not to tell anyone where she was. As a waitress, Hilga would be surrounded by people during the day.

"That's it." Molly smiled. She'd see Hilga in a few hours, shadows beneath her eyes from lack of sleep, and continuing with life onboard ship. It'd be the dark night time hours that she'd need to hide away.

Molly prayed for safety and strength. Not only for herself and Lance, but for the crew and passengers. Peace drifted over her until her eyes closed and sleep overtook her.

*

Lance burst into the security office, startling a young man dozing behind a desk. "I need to speak with the SVP, Jack Morley. Right now."

"Huh?" The man slammed his feet to the floor and blinked several times.

Lance flashed his badge. "Jack Morley. Now, please."

"He's off duty. Sleeping. I'm Owen. How can I help you?"

"One of your waitresses, Hilga, intercepted this message for Molly Nicholson." Lance pulled the note from his pocket. "I'm sure you're aware of the investigation into Antonio's death?"

"Vaguely."

"Excuse me?"

Owen shrugged. "It's been classified as a suicide."

"On whose authority?"

"Morley's." Owen rolled his neck. "Look, if you have a threatening note, you can give it to me, and I'll pass it to the SVP."

"That's it?"

"Pretty much."

Lance planted his good hand on the desktop and leaned closer. "Antonio's death was not a suicide. Anyone who thinks so is an imbecile. People do not put plastic bags over their heads on purpose."

"Sure they do." Owen spun in his chair and pushed a button on the computer behind him. "I did some research. It's rare, but it happens. Most of them have some kind of gas in the bag, but maybe Antonio didn't have any on hand. It wasn't a secret how heartbroken he was."

"Of all the idiotic—" Anger simmered like water in a boiling pot, overflowing inside of Lance. He grabbed a deep breath to calm his racing pulse. He'd find Agent Cohn. Maybe he'd listen to reason. "Make a copy of the note and hand me back the original, please."

"Sure thing." Owen placed the paper on a copier

and pressed Start. A green light glowed beneath the lid. "If you want to investigate further, that's your prerogative." Once the copy was made, he handed the original back to Lance. "Good luck."

Lance whirled and stalked out of the office. Outside, he leaned against the wall and rubbed his hand over his face. Something was fishy on board the *Destiny*, and he'd be hanged if he'd leave Molly's safety in the hands of men who couldn't see the shore for the ocean.

He'd make sure Molly didn't suffer Abby's fate, or that of Antonio's. Without cooperation from security, he wasn't sure how he'd accomplish the feat, but he'd do it. With God's help. Or he'd die trying.

Fatigue dogged his steps on the way to his stateroom. Fortitude alone wouldn't make him any use to anyone unless he got some sleep. He glanced at his watch. Four hours until he had to pick up Molly. It'd have to be enough.

Why wasn't the perpetrator sending him messages? Trying to take him out of the picture? Being onboard, the perp would know Lance stayed glued to Molly's side. Getting him out of the way would clear a path to her. It didn't make sense. Maybe after some shut-eye he'd see things more clearly.

I could use some help here, God. Some clarity.

He turned the corner and almost ran into the backs of Morrison and the chief Purser, Bob Dickson. He ducked behind a pillar.

"What do you mean my account is empty?" Morrison's voice rang through the empty corridor.

"Lower your voice, please. Guests are sleeping."

"I will not lower my voice! I've been robbed.

Someone needs to look into it. You're obviously mistaken."

"It's exactly what I said," Bob explained, "you'll need to transfer funds from somewhere. There isn't enough for you to pay for this cruise. If the money isn't there by five p.m. today, we'll set you off at the next port."

"You can't do that!" Morrison's hands balled into fists. "Someone will pay for this."

Morrison out of money? Lance gnawed the inside of his cheek. What about the funds he supposedly embezzled? Did Cohn know about this? Did the FBI freeze Morrison's assets? Lance knew from experience a man backed into a corner was a dangerous one. If Morrison was the killer and Molly his target, the threat had escalated.

"What's going on here?"

Lance peeked to see the SVP striding down the hall.

"The credit card Mr. Morrison is using for expenses on this cruise has been denied. We'll have no other option than to leave him at port."

"I'll handle this, Bob. You can go back to your post." Jack Morley gripped Morrison's arm. "This is not the place to do this. Come with me."

Lance kept the pillar between him and the two men, stepping into the open when they'd marched past. His gut told him something bigger than an empty bank account was at the bottom of Morrison having no money. He intended to find out what. In the meantime, he'd keep whatever information he dug up between him and Cohn.

The two men disappeared around the corner. By the time Lance rounded the turn in the hall, they were nowhere in sight. The arrow above the elevator glowed.

He rubbed his sleep-deprived eyes. Once he safely deposited Molly in the dining room, he'd hunt down Cohn.

CYNTHIA HICKEY

15

Molly opened the door. Lance stood there looking like an unwanted dog. Hair stuck up straight on his head, whiskers colored his jaw line and chin, and red rimmed his eyes. "Did you get any sleep?"

"About two hours." Lance stepped aside to allow her to exit the cabin. "I'll be fine."

"I only got four hours, but man, you look terrible."

"Thanks." He reached around her and pulled the door closed. "Way to build up a guy's self-esteem."

"Sorry." Molly tilted her head. Like he needed a boost in that department. Somehow, she didn't think he suffered too much from low self-esteem. "Where do you want to go first?"

"Did I miss something?" Lance blinked repeatedly. "Don't you have work to do?"

"Not until we find Hilga." That should be a no-brainer. At the forefront of his detective mind. "The ship docks in two hours. If we don't find her by then, there's no telling where she is. Kidnapped, maybe. Shanghaied. Dragged from the boat and dumped overboard."

Lance ran his hand through his hair, making it more disarrayed, and cuter than any man had a right to be.

"You watch too many movies. She could've spent the night with her boyfriend."

"I've considered that. If she did, we'll see her at breakfast." Molly gave him what she hoped was a 'cut-it-out-and be-serious' look. "You need some coffee to soften your mood. Dining room first." She headed in that direction as fast as her legs would carry her and prayed Hilga would be there, towering over the pastry bar, blond hair shoved beneath a hair net.

Muted conversation greeted her from the half-full dining room. Warm mouth-watering aromas of sausage and maple syrup welcomed her stomach and alerted her to the fact she hadn't eaten since lunch the day before. Hilga was nowhere to be seen. Molly's heart sank. "She's not here."

"Take some pictures. Ask the other crew members a few questions. Act normal. I'll be at the back table with Agent Cohn." Lance strolled toward the back of the room and chose the last empty seat at the table where Cohn and Morrison both sat.

Molly raised her eyebrows, and then quickly turned away before she alerted the two men to Lance's reason for choosing that particular table. Like Daniel in the lion's den. At least that's what it looked like to her. FBI agent or not, Cohn's heavy forehead and deep-set eyes made him look mean.

Morrison could be the nicest guy on the planet, but his salt-and-pepper hair made him suspicious right out of the gate. Especially since that was all they knew of the man in the photo. What could a one-armed Lance do if trouble rose?

She scanned the dining room and counted at least fifteen men with the same color hair as Morrison. Were they focusing on the wrong man? Just because he was suspected for embezzling didn't make him a murderer. No. She shook her head. Her gut told her he was the guilty one. She'd stick to that assumption unless proven wrong.

She marched toward the buffet line. An Asian man, only a couple of inches taller than her five-foot-two-inches, cut thick slices of ham. "Excuse me? Have you seen Hilga?"

"No. She not here."

"Have you seen her today?"

"I say no. You not understand English?" He waved her away. "She no show up. Go away. I busy."

Molly bit her lip and glanced at Lance. He seemed to concentrate on the plate in front of him. Would he see her if she slipped out? She couldn't stand around doing nothing when Hilga could be in danger. Lance chose to concentrate on Cohn and Morrison. Standing around would drive her nuts. Every minute counted. They needed to search the ship.

She studied the rest of the crew members before approaching a dark-skinned girl with waist-length hair. Molly pulled a piece of paper from her camera bag, scribbled a note, and held it to the young woman. "See that man over there? The one with a sling? Could you give him this, please?"

"Sure. I'd be glad to. He's cute." The girl winked, then sashayed toward Lance's table.

Molly rolled her eyes and slipped from the dining room. She paused in the Grand Foyer and allowed her gaze to roam the stairs heading upward. Which deck should she start on? Inside or outside? There were too many choices in a floating apartment building.

Lance appeared at her elbow. "Where are we headed?"

"No one has seen Hilga. I don't know where to start." The panic intensified, churning in her stomach. "I should've been a better friend. Found out her likes and dislikes. Then I might know where to start looking."

"You've known her less than a week, Molly. Don't put that burden on yourself. Let's think. When she left us last night, she wore her uniform. White shorts and a red shirt. Gym shoes on her feet." Lance rubbed his chin. "Common attire for dress at sea, but the red, white, and blue of Midnight Cruise Lines' colors might set her apart."

"How did you remember all that?" Molly glanced at the navy shirt she'd slept in. Wrinkles criss-crossed the front. The shorts were just as bad. She'd need to change before the purser saw her. What did her hair look like? She raised a hand to pat down her curls.

"It's my business to remember details." Lance tucked her arm through his. "Let's stroll outside. Clear our heads. We might think of something we've missed."

"Spencer!" Cohn jogged to join them. "Step over here a minute, will you? I've got to make this quick before we're seen together."

Molly glanced at Lance. He shrugged, and they moved out of sight of the dining room. No way were they leaving her behind. She followed.

Cohn crossed his arms. "Since you chose to sit at my table, I'm assuming you wanted to speak with me?"

Lance nodded. "We're missing a crew member." He explained the happenings of the night before. "This is

Molly Nicholson, the missing woman's roommate. She's also been receiving threats."

Molly's heart sank with each word. Hearing it again reinforced her feeling that Hilga was in trouble. She planted fists on her hips and stepped in front of the agent. "What are you going to do about all this, Agent Cohn? We have two people dead, a murderer running loose, and now my roommate is missing." *And I don't want to be next.*

"I'm working on it." He tilted his head. "You keep taking pictures and leave this to the law enforcement officers."

Heat rose in her face. "Excuse me?" She leaned until her face was inches from his chest. She tilted her chin. "This concerns me. I'm being threatened. I will not step down and wait to be killed!"

"Come on, Molly." Lance snaked an arm around her waist.

"Before you leave, Spencer," Cohn eyed Molly a moment, and then transferred his attention to Lance, "I think your friend may have gone overboard."

"What?" Molly pulled free of Lance's hold. "Why would you think that?"

"Before breakfast, I heard a scream. Didn't think much about it really. There's a lot of noise on a cruise ship." Cohn dug in his pocket and pulled out a swatch of red cotton. "When I went outside, I didn't see anything at first. I lit a cigarette and leaned against the railing. This fluttered a few inches over the side. Does it look familiar?"

Molly took the scarlet scrap. "It looks like it could be from Hilga's uniform top. So, instead of looking for the source of the scream, you smoked?"

"While I searched, Miss Nicholson." He narrowed his eyes. "There was nothing to see. No alarm had been sounded. No reason, until now, to think anyone had gone over."

Her throat burned from unshed tears. Poor Hilga. "We need to tell the captain." She whirled and dashed toward the elevator.

*

"Molly!" Lance caught up with her at the elevators. Her shoulders shook with silent sobs.

"She's gone overboard. Pushed."

He pulled her hands away from her face and pulled her to his chest. "It'll be all right." He rubbed her back in circular motions to stop her shudders. "We don't know that anything happened to her."

"Stop saying that!" She pulled free and glared up at him with a red, tear-streaked face. "Stop saying we don't know. We do!" She jabbed a finger into his chest. "Look me in the eye and tell me you don't believe she got thrown overboard, or that something equally as bad happened to her."

"I can't." He struggled to keep his gaze locked on hers when all he wanted to do was look away. Her pain cut a raw path through his soul.

"See, you think the same thing." Molly's knees buckled.

Lance caught her and lowered her into a nearby chair. He knelt and took her hand in his. "You're right. I'm sorry. I do think something has happened to her." Molly's hands trembled. "But I didn't want you to worry more than you needed to."

"Worry?" Her eyes widened. "I'm terrified! If you weren't with me all the time, I'd be shark bait right now. Instead, Antonio and Hilga are gone. Not to mention the stranger in the warehouse. How many more, Lance? Huh?"

"It won't happen to you, Molly. I promise." He'd do everything in his power to make sure he kept that promise. Die, if he had to. He rubbed the tears from her face. God wouldn't do that to him. Take the life of two women in his care. He refused to entertain the thought.

"You can't make that kind of promise." She rose and pulled her hand free. "Let's go see the captain."

When she stormed away it was like she sapped the warmth out of the room. A frigid fist seized Lance's heart and squeezed. Molly had adopted a spirit of despair. They should've prayed. Now, she stood with slumped shoulders beside the elevator.

Lord, don't let me fail her. If he had any solid evidence to make an accusation, he'd haul the suspect in for questioning at the next port. But he didn't. Now, a woman might be dead. The question is, why Hilga? What was her connection? The note she'd received from the boy in the arcade wasn't enough to kill her, was it?

And, the next name on the killer's list could be Molly.

CYNTHIA HICKEY

16

Molly waited in the Grand Foyer for Lance to shower and change. He'd kicked up a fuss, but finally relented when she said she ought to be safe enough in plain sight of the passengers.

Her photographer's eye noted the flushed, expectant faces of those leaving the ship. She couldn't help but snap their pictures. *Lord, why did You get me this job only to have it become a nightmare? I'm a good photographer. Great, in fact. Your word says You give us the desires of our heart. Isn't this my desire? What am I missing?*

She blinked back tears and moved outside to the railing, stepping on the first rung in order to get a better shot, and lifted the Nikon. She adjusted the aperture. "Up here!"

She waved to the honeymoon couple she'd seen on her first day. Still dressed as twins, they glanced up and waved. Molly clicked the shutter button. She'd love to follow them around and chronicle their honeymoon trip. See whether love really amounted to what people said it did.

"There you are." Lance laid a hand on her lower back. "Could you step back, please?"

"Sorry." Molly climbed down.

He'd combed his hair, shaved, and splashed on more of his trademark cologne. Her back tingled where his hand rested. Maybe there was something to this love thing after all? She hated to think magnetism and infatuation ruled the hearts of mankind. Especially when a man with a crooked grin smiled down at her.

"Hey, where's your sling?" Instead of the usual dark blue canvas encasing his arm, she spotted the black vinyl strap of a backpack.

"Took it off." His hand moved to wrap around her waist. "Can't teach you self-defense with it on."

"Are you supposed to have it off?"

He steered her toward the gangplank. "Yes, mother. I'll be fine. It's been several weeks. The wound is healing nicely, according to Dr. Max, who told me to start using it. The shot was what they call a 'through and through'. I'll live."

"Won't you need physical therapy?" Molly glanced up at him, liking the familiar way he kept her close. She'd enjoy Lance while she could. He'd already take a piece of her with him when the cruise ended.

"What beach would you like to go to?"

Molly shrugged. "Okay. I can take a hint. Change of subject. According to the guidebook, the main road through town is Ali Drive. It follows the coastline. We'll stop when the mood strikes."

"Sounds good to me."

Within minutes, the salty mist kissed Molly's face as they drove through Kailua-Kona. A white steeple rose, stark in its simplicity, above the town. Tourists sat on the concrete embankment that held back the ocean. White sand mixed with hardened lava provided a pleasant contrast of color.

She could live among the islands, snorkeling every day, taking photos of marine life and local plants. Watching the sun set over a majestic volcano. Maybe when ship life grew boring she'd come back. Hopefully, with a loving man by her side whether God chose Lance to be her husband, or someone she hadn't met yet. Molly didn't relish settling in a romantic place alone.

"How about here?" Lance pulled the car to the side of the road.

A carpet of sand spread before them, sparkling like diamond dust beneath the sun. The azure sea lapped at the beach. "Perfect." Molly popped the latch on her door, then remembered Lance's irritation at her not waiting, and sat back.

He loped to the passenger side, flung the door wide, and swept his arm in a bow. His eyes twinkled from beneath the inky bangs falling in his eyes. "M'lady. Paradise awaits."

"Thank you, kind sir." She slid from the seat, enjoying the warmth of the day on her skin. The only thought marring the beach's tranquility was their purpose for being there. Instead of playing in the surf like tourists, she'd learn self-defense. Her trip to Hawaii didn't turn out as planned.

Nothing to do about it, but persevere. She followed Lance to the water's edge and laid her camera case next to his backpack, before kicking off her shoes and shedding her outer clothing. The sand was powder beneath her bare feet.

"Race you to the water!"

She dashed away at Lance's shout.

A few sunbathers lay spread on colorful beach

towels. Others carried snorkeling gear or body boards into the water. Molly splashed in up to her waist.

"You cheated." Lance plowed through the surf. The scar from his wound pink against his tanned skin.

Molly averted her eyes away from his muscled physique. How would she be able to concentrate? She sighed. "Okay, what's first?"

"First, I tell you some things you can do. Please don't try them on me." He winked. "They aren't pleasant."

She crossed her arms and raised her eyebrows. "Do tell." This might be fun after all.

"The elbow jab you gave me was good. Here's another move if the assailant is behind you." Lance wrapped his arm around her neck. Molly's nerves tingled at his closeness. He smelled of sea air, and suntan lotion. "Grab the uh…groin area as hard as possible, and yank upwards. Believe me that hurts."

She giggled. "Experienced it first hand, have you?"

"No, but I've seen it done." He faced her. "If your assailant is in front of you, take the palm of your hand," he grabbed her right hand, spread her fingers and moved her arm up. "And thrust upward on the nose, shoving the bone into the brain."

She shivered and hoped no one got close enough for her to use the techniques. She'd rather run.

"There's always the two fingers to the eyes. And, if you're feeling particularly strong—" He leaped behind her, grabbed her arm, thrust his hip against her pelvis, and tossed her over his shoulder, dunking her.

Salt water filled her nose, and she rose to the surface, sputtering. "You could've given me some warning!"

"An assailant won't. The element of surprise will be your greatest weapon, Molly." Lance crossed his arms, cocked his eyebrows, and grinned slyly. "Now you try to flip me."

"No." She struggled to reach the shore.

"What's wrong?" Lance followed. "I thought you wanted to do this?"

"I do." She thrust her hip into his abdomen, bent, and flung him over her shoulder. She probably should've told him she grew up with male cousins and tended to pick up self-defense moves quickly. Within seconds, he lay on the sand, breath knocked from him, while she laughed down at him. "Just wanted the element of surprise."

He resembled a living statue portraying the epitome of man. Molly turned before he could read the emotions on her face. How could she even think of a man after her disastrous relationship with Vince? Inconceivable. Or was it? Maybe her time with Vince was so she'd know the real thing when she saw it.

*

She was a fast learner. Lance's laugh escaped him in a wheeze, then shut off as if someone had flicked a switch. The sun highlighted Molly's slicked back hair with gold. Water glistened from her skin like jewels. White teeth flashed from between rose-colored lips.

He yanked her down and claimed her mouth with his, tasting the salt from the sea. She stiffened, then relaxed, matching his ardor. Lance gentled his actions, pulling her against him and moving to nuzzle her neck. When her lack of breath matched his, he released her. "How's that for surprise?"

Her eyes widened. "Not funny!" She rose and

kicked sand at him, coating his wet skin.

He couldn't help it. She'd looked so lovely standing over him. A vision from heaven to light up his world. Less than five days and he was hooked as badly as the heroin addicts he busted back home. Molly was a drug he didn't want rehabilitated out of his system. He propped his upper body on an elbow.

She strolled along the shore, red one-piece bathing suit accentuating rather than hiding her feminine curves. She might be petite, but Molly Nicholson screamed woman. Lance shook his head. He'd been an idiot in the past, focusing his attentions on women he'd thought had class and style. Molly put them all to shame.

Breathing back to normal, he rose and jogged down the beach to her side. When he reached her, he took her hand in his. They strolled in silent communication more eloquent than any words. Lance's heart hitched. He loved Molly Nicholson. No way would he allow her to walk away at the end of the cruise.

"Do you think Hilga was dead before being tossed overboard? Maybe that wasn't her that screamed." Molly's whisper cut through the silence. "Passengers goof around all the time. Maybe some kids were playing. I'd hate for her to have had the fear of drowning."

"We can hope so." Lance squeezed her hand. Despite her quick willingness to smile, he knew Molly's heart carried a weight of fear. He'd give anything to lessen her burden. *Lord, show me what to do.*

Sure, his presence would deter danger, but for how long? Desperate people tended to take desperate measures. He hadn't found any new clues since protecting Molly. Should he just leave things to Cohn? He was on vacation, after all. Sitting back and letting the FBI handle things on their own, assume responsibility for deaths that occurred onboard, would prevent him from stretching himself too thin. Leaving him strengthened to protect Molly. He itched to investigate further. No, he wouldn't drag Molly around while he searched for her friend. His investigating would have to be done at night after she returned to her cabin.

He couldn't not do it. It wasn't in him to sit back while people died. Always the desire to play hero ran through his veins. Even as a child when he'd rescue every stray animal that crossed his path. Somehow, he'd help Cohn and keep Molly safe at the same time. God willing.

CYNTHIA HICKEY

17

Molly slicked Firebomb lipstick on her lips, then stepped back to study her reflection in the mirror. The cocktail dress flowed around her knees when she moved. The front plunged enough to be alluring, yet still remain modest. The back draped in graceful folds to her waist. Her hair lay in a smooth bob, the curls tamed. At least for now. Around her neck, she wore a simple diamond teardrop to match the ones in her ears.

"Not bad." She smiled, knowing she'd leave Lance speechless. The thought gave her a chill. For the first time in a long time, she felt beautiful. Looked beautiful. After clipping her I.D. badge to her waist, she slung her camera over her shoulder.

Lance's familiar, one-two-one-two-three knock sounded. With one more smile in the mirror, Molly answered the door.

If she thought she'd knock his socks off, he sent her spiraling into outer space. Lance leaned against the door jamb. His inky hair was slicked back and a dark Armani tuxedo covered his muscular frame. A cologne, smelling of the night and the sea, assaulted her, sending her senses reeling.

His lip curled, causing his dimple to flash. "If you

don't close your mouth, beautiful, a fly will get in."

She closed it quick as a snapping turtle. And she thought he'd be the speechless one. "Aren't you conceited?" Her gaze scanned him from head to toe. Laughter burst from her and she pointed at the price tag dangling from his sleeve. "Two hundred dollars?"

His face reddened as he pulled the tag free. "It was the cheapest I could find."

"I'm not laughing at the price, silly. Just the fact you left it on." She tucked her arm in his. "You weren't planning on returning it after the cruise were you?"

"Maybe." He laid a hand on the small of her back. "You look stunning."

"So do you." If she thought his looks sent her flying, his touch sling-shotted her to another galaxy. She gulped a deep breath to control her breathing.

"Do you think we could get someone to take our picture tonight?"

His gaze focused on her with such intensity, all moisture left her mouth.

Molly peered into his face, stunned by the soft look in his eyes. Could he possibly care for her as much as she did him? She should stop and pray about the situation before she found herself in another heartbreak. "I think that can be arranged."

At least she'd have something to remember him by when he left. The thought threatened to steal the evening's enjoyment and sent her heart to the pit of her stomach.

Lance leaned closer and peered into her face. "What's wrong?"

She forced a smile to her face. "Nothing."

His expression told her he didn't believe her, but

decided to let the matter lie. Lance opened the door to the dining room and they entered into an atmosphere of muted conversation, candlelight, and the quiet presence of waiters. Mouth watering aromas of prime beef and seafood greeted them.

A feeling of enchantment filled the air on the cruise's first formal night. Passengers filled the dining room, decked out in their finery. Women were clothed in gowns in every hue of the rainbow. The men's attire ranged from suits to tuxedos, but in Molly's opinion, none of them matched the grandeur of Lance. She stood taller entering the room at his side. He placed a kiss on her forehead and slid away to claim an empty chair at the nearest table.

Molly smoothed the skirt of her dress and lifted her camera before moving to an elderly couple holding hands on top of a crisp white tablecloth. "Photograph?"

They nodded. "Tilt your heads together, just a little bit, and smile like you're sharing a secret." Molly grinned. "Perfect." She snapped the shutter button and moved to the next couple.

Contributing to the pleasurable experience of others lifted her spirits; until she turned and caught the icy stare of Robert Morrison from across the room. Her skin crawled as if millions of tiny spiders trekked up and down its surface. She sought out Lance. A few yards away, he watched her over the rim of his water glass. He nodded, and she relaxed. While in his sights, nothing could happen to her. Let Morrison stare. She wouldn't give him the satisfaction of seeing her fear.

Molly returned to her job and did her best to ignore the man. Instead, she felt his gaze burn a hole in the back of her head. Always there, leaving a mark while she traveled from passenger to passenger. Like a predator waiting for the opportunity to pounce.

Daniella circulated the other side of the room, snapping pictures. Molly worked her way around to her co-worker. She wanted a photo of her and Lance on deck with the moon rising behind them. "Daniella?"

"Hey, Molly." Her grin faded. "Sorry to hear about Hilga. Very tragic."

"Yeah." Molly sighed. "What did you hear?"

"That she jumped." Daniella scooted closer. "Her boyfriend is devastated. Said he had no idea she was suicidal."

Molly chewed the inside of her lip. Hilga didn't jump anymore than Antonio tied a bag around his face. What was wrong with these people? "I'm wondering if you'd be willing to take a picture of Lance and me on deck?"

"Sure. Give me ten minutes."

*

Lance sipped his ice water and watched Morrison's gaze follow Molly. The intense stare turned Lance's stomach to stone. He wanted nothing more than to leave his post and smash the creep's face in.

Although Molly flitted from table to table, her too-wide smile and the way she fiddled with her hair told him Morrison's attention frightened her. Almost as much as the way she looked in that little black dress scared Lance.

When she answered the door to her cabin, he thought his heart had stopped. He'd wanted to grab her in his arms and kiss her until she was nothing more than putty. He set his glass on the table and swallowed the chuckle. Thankfully, she'd noticed the price tag he'd overlooked. So much for being Detective Observant. Not to mention his ego taking a hit.

The arrival of his filet mignon didn't draw his attention away from the vision she made. Lord, he had it bad. Falling hard for a woman was the last thing he expected when ordered to take a vacation. What would they do when he went back to work, and she continued traveling?

The woman next to him placed a hand on his arm. "What's bothering you son?"

Lance turned to face the gray-haired woman. A kind smile radiated from her wrinkled face. "Why do you ask?"

"You look like you're carrying the weight of the world on your shoulders." She nodded toward Molly. "It wouldn't have anything to do with that lovely girl you're staring at, would it?"

At least she hadn't asked about the tragic occurrences onboard. "Yes, ma'am. It might."

The woman's husband leaned across his wife. "I'm Dick, this is Jane."

Lance stared at the couple. Honestly?

The old guy grinned and shook a finger at Lance. "No smart aleck comments now." He crossed his arms on the table. His craggy face open and caring. "Tell us what the problem is. We're celebrating our fiftieth wedding anniversary. Now, that may not make us experts, but we probably have a word of wisdom to bestow on a young man such as yourself."

"I'm Lance Spencer. Problem is, I work on the mainland. The woman I find myself falling in love with, works on a cruise ship. Under contract." He straightened his utensils. "I'm not sure how a relationship between us will work."

"Are you a believer, son?" Jane patted his hand.

"Yes, ma'am."

"Have you prayed about this? Have you asked God's will concerning a relationship with this young lady?"

"Not exactly." Leave it up to a kindly stranger to point out something he should've known himself. Lance shook his head and lifted his knife and fork to cut into his steak. Prayer could've saved him a lot of heartache. What if God said no to Molly? What if she wasn't the one for him? Could he turn and walk away?

"Don't struggle with this, son." Jane gave him another pat then removed her hand. "Give it up. God can handle this."

"Yes, ma'am, I will." Lance dug into his steak with a renewed spirit. God could handle his love for Molly and the danger that surrounded her. *Lord, speak to her heart as you have spoken to mine.*

Jack Morley entered the room, his white uniform jacket pristine and pressed. He stopped and surveyed the room, before heading toward the captain's table.

"Excuse me, please." Lance nodded to his new friends, tossed his napkin on his plate, and rushed to the meet the SVP. "Morley!"

"Mr. Spencer." Jack squared his shoulders.

"Have you discovered any news on the whereabouts of Hilga?"

"No. Best we can determine is she'd gone overboard. Probably jumped. Without knowing the time or location, we've no way of finding her." He tugged on the bottom of his jacket and glanced over Lance's shoulder. "Most likely she'll wash ashore in a day or two."

"Does this happen often?"

"What?" Jack's gaze finally met his.

Was that a flicker of alarm?

"The disappearance and death of crew members. Seems common onboard the *Destiny*." Lance clapped the other man on the shoulder. "Your marketing department might want to put a warning in your next brochure."

Molly appeared at his side and glanced from Morley to him. "Daniella will take our picture."

"Wonderful." He placed an arm around her waist and steered her from the room. As they stepped out the door, he glanced back over his shoulder. Morrison continued to stare.

What was that old adage? If looks could kill.

18

Lights from the ship blocked the stars, leaving the sky a flat expanse of ebony velvet. The moon rose above the gently rolling ocean, tipping the waves with silver.

Molly leaned her elbows on the rail and sighed. No camera could capture this beauty. The picture would be nothing more than a cheap imitation of God's handiwork. She turned in the circle of Lance's arm and smiled, ready for Daniella to capture their likeness for eternity.

"You two make a great couple. Tall, dark, and handsome. Petite and fair. Just lovely." Daniella held up a finger. "Freeze. I'm taking two to make sure they turn out all right."

Heat rose to Molly's cheeks as Lance squeezed her waist. He bent and put his lips to her ear. "Tonight's the night for romance." He straightened, waved Daniella off with a thanks, and wrapped his arms around Molly. "Let's make the most of it."

Her heart leaped into her throat as he pulled her close and swayed to the music drifting from the open doors of the nightclub on a deck above them. Lance laid his cheek against her hair, and Molly breathed deep the scent of him.

She wanted him to kiss her because he wanted to, not as camouflage against anyone watching. The direction her thoughts wandered shocked her, but not as much as the revelation that Vince's abuse hadn't affected her ability to feel again. She thought she'd been broken beyond repair.

Tears sprang to her eyes as she accepted the gift God gave her. The gift of a heart still capable of emotion.

"I spoke with a wonderful old couple at dinner. They were full of wisdom." Lance's chest rumbled. "They told me to pray about how we could work out a relationship between the two of us."

He wanted a relationship with her? Molly's spirit soared.

"I'll know it'll be hard with you sailing and me on the mainland, but we can do this. See where it takes us. If you want?"

She pulled back and searched his face. "You would do that for me? Wait until the ship docked and my contract was fulfilled?"

Lance squeezed her close; his body firm against hers. Safe in its solidarity. "In a heartbeat, Molly Nicholson."

She allowed the music to move her, and kept her face against his chest, content to listen to the rhythm of his heart.

"Well? Do you want to see where this thing goes?" Lance held her at arm's length. "You haven't said."

"I would love to." Molly leaned her elbows back on the railing and stared at the water moving past the ship. "But I haven't heard much good about long distance relationships. We haven't known each other long enough to build a foundation."

"God's all the foundation we need." Lance leaned with his back against the rail. His teeth flashed white against his tanned face.

She shrugged. "My faith is new. I don't know what to expect from God." Except unconditional love. She gleaned that message from the small amount of Bible verses she'd read and grabbed hold of. But bad things happened. Even in the Bible. She wished she shared Lance's confidence in their success. Fulfilling an eight month contract at sea would be difficult enough without a man like him waiting on shore.

He smoothed back a wayward strand of hair from where it had gotten stuck in her lipstick. The slight touch sent bolts of electricity through her. Her flesh tingled. Maybe it was the romantic setting that lit her nerves on fire. She'd heard many times about shipboard romances. Especially among the crew.

Could her attraction to Lance be superficial? An infatuation for a man who protected her from danger? Once the threat against her was over, would they feel the same about each other? Did she want to chance it?

"Are you okay?" Lance cupped her cheek. She leaned into his palm.

"I'm fine. Enjoying the night … and the company." She turned her gaze back to the sea.

Something floated far below them. Molly squinted, then climbed to the first rail and leaned over. "What is that?" She turned to look at him. "Is that a person? Debris?"

Lance yanked her back to the deck. "Oh, God, help them." He whirled and grabbed a life preserver from the nearby wall then tossed it into the water. "Stay here and keep an eye on that preserver. Try not to let it out of your sight."

She nodded as he dashed into the foyer, then turned back to watch the bobbing red and white circle below her. If it was a person in the water, they weren't grabbing for the preserver. Instead, they bounced up and down like a piece of driftwood. "Grab a hold! Can you hear me?" Hilga? Molly peered without blinking until her eyes burned. She couldn't tell. Please, God.

"What's happening?" A man and woman joined her. The woman gasped. Soon a small crowd gathered around Molly and another life preserver joined the first after someone tossed the ring overboard. A couple of minutes later, the body disappeared under the ship.

*

Lance banged on the security office door, shouted the alarm, then headed back to the dining room where he'd spotted the captain earlier. Thankfully, he still sat at his table, raising a glass of wine toward the lovely woman sitting beside him. Lance laid a hand on the captain's shoulder. "Sir, may I speak with you a moment? It's urgent."

"Certainly, Mr. Spencer." Captain Barker stood and nodded to his guests. "Please excuse me." He followed Lance back to the foyer.

"It appears we may have a body overboard."

"Excuse me?" Captain Barker's skin faded beneath his tan.

"Come with me. I'll explain on the way." Lance hotfooted back in the direction of the deck with the captain keeping pace. "There's someone in the water. I tossed over a life preserver and have someone standing by to keep it in sight. I'm pretty sure it's a body, sir."

The captain's eyes widened, and he sprinted toward the door as he pulled a two-way radio from his pocket. "This is Captain Barker. Meet me on the lower deck. Have a motor boat ready. We have a search and rescue."

"I'll meet you down there." Lance returned to where he'd left Molly, surprised to find a group of people leaning over the rail.

"They've gone under." Molly turned wide eyes in his direction.

Lance gripped her arm. "Come on. The captain's sending out a boat." From the clothes the body wore, Lance had a possible identity. The mystery of where Hilga went was most likely solved. Now, they needed to find out whether she jumped or was pushed. He suspected the latter, and had no idea how to prove it.

By the time they reached the captain and SVP, along with a couple of other crew members, a motor boat had been lowered into the ocean. One of the security staff roared away in the direction where the life preservers bobbed. Those waiting huddled in silent groups. Molly rested her head on Lance's chest.

Thirty minutes later, the man arrived back on ship with something covered in a bright blue tarp.

Lance led Molly to a nearby chair. "Wait here."

"Why?"

"Please." When she nodded, he stood next to the captain. The security officer's arms trembled as he carried his burden then laid it at the captain's feet. His voice shook. "It's the waitress, Hilga, sir. There isn't much left of her. Nothing below the waist anyway. Looks like some marine life got to her. Most likely a shark."

Captain Barker rubbed his hands over his face. "Good Lord, help us. The poor girl."

Lance swallowed. There'd be little chance of proving foul play. He glanced to where Molly sat. Her wide-eyed gaze flicked from him to the tarp covered lump. Could he get away with lying? Tell her it's something other than her friend?

"As far as the passengers are concerned, the body floating in the water was a training dummy." The captain speared them all with a sharp look. The SVP stared unblinking at him, then over to where a crowd had gathered. Several of the ship's crew held them back. "Under no circumstances are they to be told the truth. That goes for the little lady sitting over there. Got it?"

Lance nodded. Problem solved, although the lie would taste bitter rolling across his tongue. From the stricken look on Molly's face, she held on to her nerves by a strand. He sat beside her and placed an arm around her shoulders.

"It's a training dummy. Used for CPR and stuff. Most likely someone's idea of a joke."

"Really?" She took a shuddering breath. "I could've sworn it was Hilga. I'm so relieved."

Lance hugged her and closed his eyes against the lie. *Forgive me, Lord.* But he'd do anything to protect her, even tell a white lie. At least for the time being. Eventually, he'd come clean. There was no reason for him to frighten her further. "Come on." He rose and took her hand. "Let's enjoy what's left of this evening. There's dancing somewhere on this ship, right?"

"Yes." Her eyes sparkled. "There's ballroom dancing."

"Perfect. I cut a mean Salsa." He stepped back in a quick one-two step.

"Try and keep up, hero. I've been dancing with my father since I was six."

Lance laughed as they strolled. Relieved to see some of the stress melt from her face.

As they entered the Grand Foyer, he scanned the faces of the milling passengers. Murmurs of the drowned dummy floated around the room. Morrison leaned in a corner, his lips twisted in a sneer.

19

Molly lay on her bed and stared at the ceiling. Today was Sunday. The ship would dock in Lahaina and by the time Molly re-boarded in the afternoon, she'd have a new cabin mate. No time to mourn during a cruise it seemed.

Although she gave Lance an A for effort at distracting her earlier with the promise of dancing, she didn't buy his story of the tarp-covered practice dummy. She knew Hilga's body lay under that covering. She'd caught a glimpse of blond hair. Who would be next? It wasn't safe for anyone to be around her. From now on, she'd be a loner, accompanied by no one but Lance. Everyone close to her died. She was worse than the plague.

"And feeling sorry for myself accomplishes nothing." She beat a fist into the mattress.

The Midnight Cruise killer, as she'd chosen to call the unknown person, was as predatory as a cat. No clues left behind, just Morrison's general creepiness. He was too obvious as the culprit. Maybe the man was generally ill-tempered. Which meant, it could possibly be someone she couldn't put a name to.

She flopped to her side. Sleep continued to elude her. Her thoughts strayed to Lance. He danced like he'd been doing it all his life, easily leading her in the steps of the Salsa. She felt safer in his arms than anywhere else on the ship.

Did she want to pursue a relationship with him?

Yes, she did. She'd known him for five days, and he occupied her heart and mind.

If not for his offer of protection, she would've only given the handsome man a cursory glance, and then continued on her way. Could his presence on the ship be God's provision? She rolled to her other side and punched her pillow. Couldn't He have chosen a better way to introduce her to a man?

Did the killer have a gun? Weapons weren't allowed onboard, without a license. Not even pepper spray. How was she supposed to defend herself? By brute strength? Not likely. Not even with the little self-defense she now knew.

She glanced at the alarm clock. Three a.m. She groaned. Sunday, her day off, she could sleep until seven and still be ready when Lance picked her up at eight. A whole day in Lahaina without working. A day to play tourist.

Good grief. Molly tossed back the thin sheet and sat up. Sleep didn't plan on arriving anytime soon. Not with the way her mind flitted from one subject to the next. She glanced at the coffee pot. Empty. She couldn't leave the room. Too dangerous, plus Lance would have her head. She flopped back and closed her eyes. Sleep would come if she had to force it!

A pounding on the door startled her awake. Molly glanced at the clock. Eight! "Hold on." She slid from the bed, donned her robe, and pressed an eye to the door's peephole. Lance grinned back at her, and she whipped the door open. "I'm so sorry. You woke me. Give me fifteen minutes."

"I've never known a woman to be ready in that amount of time, but okay. I'll wait out here." He shoved a mug of coffee in her hand. "This will help."

"You're a Godsend." She flashed him a smile and closed the door before breathing in the heady aroma. Ambrosia!

She took a few sips, then rushed to shower. When she emerged from her cabin at 8:20, Lance glanced at his watch. "Only five minutes late. I'm impressed. Ready for breakfast?"

"Yes, I'm starving."

"Do you want to eat here or on shore?"

"Let's eat the Continental breakfast. It'll be fast." Molly led the way to an upper deck, entered the dining room, and joined the buffet line. The tinkle of silverware and clanking of plates mingled with the drone of the passengers' conversations. She inhaled the sweet scent of muffins and cinnamon rolls. After filling her plate with scrambled eggs and pastries, she chose a table in the back of the room.

Lance paused beside her. "Switch seats with me."

"Why?"

"It's a cop thing. I like to see the room and who enters."

Molly's fork clattered to her plate. "Makes sense." She rose and sat in the other chair, then scooted closer to Lance. Having her back to the room gave her the heebie-jeebies. Besides, there were worse things than sitting close to the man. He certainly smelled delicious.

Lance set his plate on the table and winked at her. Heat flooded her face. Let him think what he liked. If it was a relationship he wanted, then that's what he'd get. Despite her embarrassment, she grinned up at him and forked in a mouthful of eggs.

*

Lance loved the way Molly's cheeks flushed when he teased her. She'd informed him the night before she was off duty today. He planned to act like a love-struck couple as they strolled the streets of Lahaina. Of course, with all the cars he'd rented, this vacation cost more than he'd budgeted for. He ducked his head to hide a smile as he thought of their mode of travel for the day.

"What's so funny?" Molly wiped her mouth, then tossed her napkin on the table.

"Nothing." Lance stood and offered her a hand. "Ready?"

He ushered her out of the room and down the gangplank ahead of him, then stood back to gauge her reaction when she spotted the metallic-blue motorcycle parked at the curb. Her eyes lit up and she clapped her hands.

"Seriously?"

"I thought riding to the top of Haleakala Crater might be more fun on one of these."

"It will be grand. You did read about the road to Hana, right?"

"Oh, yeah. Six hundred curves and fifty-four one-lane bridges. Half this side of the crater, half the other side." Lance rubbed his hands together. "I can't wait. Is Hana okay? I figured we could visit Lahaina tomorrow and hit the more adventurous sites today, when you're free."

"I think that's a wonderful idea." She grabbed a pink metallic helmet, put it on, then clasped the buckle under her chin. "I've never ridden on a motorcycle before. Let's go!"

"Never?" Maybe this wasn't such a good idea.

"No, but I'll hold on real tight." She winked and slung a leg over the seat. "What are you waiting for?"

Good Lord, save them. Lance donned his black helmet, took his seat in front, then gunned the engine. They roared away from the dock. He drove down Highway 30 then switched onto highways with names he couldn't pronounce. Looming in the distance, deceptively farther than it appeared, rose the mighty *House of the Sun*. He only wished they'd been able to view the sunrise from the crater's summit.

The ocean breeze washed across his face and arms with the refreshing scent of salt and sea. Molly kept both arms wrapped around his middle. He couldn't think of a better place to be. He could die a happy man right now. Sun, wind, surf, and Molly's arms wrapped around his waist.

The ocean pounded at the bottom of a sheer cliff to their right. The lush jungle rose on their left, sprinkled with miniature waterfalls. Molly laid her cheek on his back and squeezed. If Lance's grin got any bigger, his face would split.

After an hour, they veered off the Highway, passing pineapple fields and farmland to begin their ascent to the crater.

*

When she wasn't relishing the feel of Lance's strong back against her cheek, Molly swiveled her head from side to side, trying in vain to take in all the scenic view surrounding her. The trees thinned as they headed toward the top of the crater.

By the time they let down the bike's kickstand, her legs wobbled and her backside had fallen asleep. The physical discomfort couldn't dim her anticipation of one of the world's rare sights.

Lance grabbed her hand and pulled her with him to the scenic overlook. He squeezed through several onlookers, pulling Molly with him. The surface of the moon spread beneath them with black sand and smaller craters. She lifted her Nikon from its case and started snapping photos. Far below them, a line of horseback riders disappeared over the horizon.

"Maybe not one of the more colorful views we've seen," Lance said. "But definitely one of the most unique."

"I think it's gorgeous." Molly moved to a part of the waist-high railing with a sheer drop on the other side.

"That's far enough." Lance stopped a few feet from the edge.

"I'll be fine." Molly lifted her camera and balanced her hips against the iron bars.

A group of people crowded around her. Her feet slipped, and she felt herself going over. Letting the camera hang from its strap around her neck, she fought for a foothold. Her foot slipped, and she fell further. "Help! Lance!"

Bile rose in her throat as bodies pressed closer, eager to catch a glimpse of the crater's bottom. She struggled to press back and regain her footing. Instead, the movement sent her over until her stomach rested on the top bar. Her heart pounded in her ears. This was it. She'd die in paradise inside a volcano.

Lance pulled her back. "This is why I don't like heights. You could fall."

She fought to catch her breath. "I didn't fall. Somebody pushed me."

CYNTHIA HICKEY

20

Are you sure?" Lance gripped her upper arms. Her skin gave under his fingers. He let up on the pressure so he wouldn't leave bruises. "Positive." Molly's wide eyes stood out in her pale face. Tears shimmered, threatening to fall. "I … distinctly felt … two hands on my back then a forceful shove."

Lance whirled and scanned the crowd. A man wearing a hooded sweatshirt jumped into a dark sedan with tinted windows and roared out of the parking lot. He'd stood two feet away and someone had the nerve to try and harm her in front of his eyes. His line of work had previously showed him the range of people's boldness, but this took the cake.

Rage boiled through his veins like the lava from the inactive Haleakala Crater. He grabbed Molly's hand. "Come on!"

"We aren't going to follow him, are we?" Molly winced as he slammed the helmet on her head. Her eyes hardened. "We are? You're crazy!"

"Maybe so, but I want to put an end to this once and for all." He clenched his jaw so tight the muscles ached. "I said I would protect you, and that's what I'm going to do. Stopping this is the best way."

"And get us killed in the meantime." She crossed her arms.

"You could've been killed back there!" Lance flung an arm wide. What was wrong with her? Couldn't she see the danger of continuing as they were? Every time she stepped out of her cabin, her life was in peril. Maybe he should just lock her in there and stand guard until they docked. She'd certainly be safer that way. "I thought you wanted to solve this."

"I do. But I don't want to die doing it."

"I won't let that happen." Not if it was in his power. He'd die first.

"Fine! But if we wind up dead, don't come whining to me." Molly climbed on the back of the motorcycle.

Lance choked back a laugh at the irony in her remark. Tilting her chin, she glared.

Fear radiated from her eyes, turning the green irises the color of the sea surrounding Maui. Seeing her almost tumble over the protective barrier had sent his heart plummeting and erased his trepidation of heights for a brief moment. Now, it raced like the engine of the bike, roaring in his ears and blocking out other sounds. He stared down the road to where the car had disappeared.

"Let's go." Molly's gaze shot daggers.

"I'm sorry." Lance wrapped his arms around her until her stiff posture relaxed. "I get … bossy, when I'm scared." And overprotective. This wasn't like any case he'd been on before. With his feelings for Molly growing, things were personal.

"That's an understatement." Her voice sounded muffled against his chest. "Let's find a place to grab lunch."

"A great idea." Lance tilted her face to his and planted a soft kiss on her lips. "Forgiven?"

"How can I stay angry when you're concerned about my welfare?" She smiled and pulled away. "Crank up this beast and let's get out of here."

*

Molly would hate to see Lance really mad if his reaction a few minutes ago was any indication of his pressure point. He'd resembled a simmering volcano. She laid her hands on the tense muscles in his shoulders. Not angry anymore, her foot. At least he hadn't raised a fist in her face. She bit her lower lip. How long would it be before she stopped comparing him to Vince? Could she really trust Lance not to raise a hand in anger toward her?

The bike vibrated under her as the beauty of Maui whipped past. They'd had to grab sightseeing and fun around tragedies. Molly sighed. So much for a job slash vacation. Look at that; run for your life. See that; run for your life. She laid her cheek against Lance's broad back. *Thank you, God, I'm not going through this alone.*

They lurched to the left, then right around the car in front of them. Lance hugged the bike against the mountain, and increased their speed. Things whipped past in a blur. Her hair slapped wildly against her back. Lance had increased their speed.

Molly's breath lodged in her throat as the rear tires sprayed gravel. Why was he driving like a lunatic? "What are you doing?"

"Trying to outrun the car on our tail!"

Peeking over her shoulder, Molly choked back a scream. The dark colored sedan they'd seen in the parking lot filled her vision. The driver wore a baseball cap pulled low over his eyes. His only discernible physical trait was a strong chin.

The car advanced until mere inches separated them.

"Hurry!" She tightened her hold around Lance's middle.

Their pursuer pulled closer until he was between them and the thick foliage. Molly glanced down at the ocean thundering against the rocks. Why weren't there barricades along the entire length of this road? There'd be no possible chance of surviving the impact. They'd burst into flames if they went over.

Lance gunned the engine and they jerked forward. Molly's feet slipped from the grips, and she almost lost her hold.

Like a souped-up navy blue beast the car swerved until its fender almost touched Molly's thigh. She screamed as the bike edged closer to the cliff.

"Hold on!" Lance yelled and shifted into a higher gear. The engine roared.

The trees and water zipped past them in a dizzy array of colors. They approached a curve in the road, with, thankfully, a metal barricade. The car closed in. The bike teetered until Molly thought they'd leave flesh on the only thing preventing them from sailing into the sea.

She lifted Lance's shirt and yanked his pistol from his waistband, keeping a firm grip around his waist with the other. With her heart in her throat, she aimed behind them and pulled the trigger. Nothing. What was wrong with the stupid thing? It looked so easy in the movies.

"What are you doing?" Lance yelled.

"Trying to make him fall back."

"The safety's on. Put the gun back where you found it before you shoot someone."

"That's the idea!"

Lance zigzagged through oncoming traffic before whipping down a road marked with an arrow pointing toward The Seven Pools.

Molly glanced back again. The sedan was stuck behind a convertible occupied by two middle-aged couples. She released a shuddering breath and let her arm fall to her side.

Several minutes later, Lance pulled the bike to a stop in a crowded parking lot. He leaped from the bike and grabbed his weapon from her hand. "And you call me crazy. Have you shot a gun before?"

"No."

Lance released his breath in a huff. "Come on. We can't stay here. We need to mix with the crowd." He grabbed her hand and pulled her along with him.

"I'm sorry." She jogged to keep up with his pace. "I thought for sure we were going over."

"There were other people on that road, Molly. What if you would've hit one of them?" A muscle twitched in his jaw.

She hadn't thought of that. The gun had poked her stomach the entire ride, reminding her of its presence. She'd done the only thing she could think of. Other than faint. "I'm sorry."

He shook his head and squeezed her hand. "It's good to know you'll react violently when your life is in danger."

She'd responded without thinking. Survival trumped fear.

They merged with a group of sightseers on tour and

hiked to the resplendent seven pools. Sunbathers lay on the emerald grass. One pool fell into another until the scene changed to a rock wall overlooking the ocean, a rainbow its crowning glory.

God's promise. Everything would be all right.

Lance laid his arm around Molly's shoulders and pulled her close to his side. He kept his right arm cradled close to his body. She'd forgotten about his injury. Fighting to keep the motorcycle upright must've been a hefty price.

"You should have the doctor look you over again when we get back."

He glanced down at her. "Why?"

"Your arm."

"It'll be fine. I need to start using it."

"In moderation, I'm sure." Molly transferred her attention back to the colored arch over their head.

Her entire life had been spent with her head down, avoiding direct contact with people. That was one reason why she'd chosen a profession as a photographer. Safety behind the lens. What she'd gone through with Vince had strengthened her. A sign of God bringing good from the bad.

She slid in front of Lance, pulling his arms around her from behind. There may only be a few more days of his company, he may only be passing the time in order to protect her, but she'd cherish every minute with the wonderful man.

He nuzzled her neck. "I don't think the man trying to run us off the road was Morrison."

"Why?"

"Because Mr. Morrison is getting cozy with a waitress from the ship." He turned Molly to face behind them.

Morrison and a girl Molly didn't know rolled around on a beach towel oblivious to the families around them. From their passionate embrace, they'd been there awhile. The girl suddenly giggled, leaped to her feet, and dashed off, Robert Morrison in hot pursuit. Molly's cheeks burned.

Lance laughed and turned back to the thundering surf. "Doesn't seem like the sour faced man we've come to know, does it?"

"If Morrison isn't the one after me, then who is?" She pulled away and scanned the thinning group of people around the pools.

No one seemed suspicious or overly concerned about her or Lance. How could she have been so wrong about Morrison? Antonio said the guy had graying hair. She stomped her foot. They needed more to go on. Wrapping her arms around her middle, she struggled to control her breathing. Having a face to put with the person threatening her was safer than an unknown assailant.

"Come on." Lance unfolded her arms and entwined the fingers of his left hand with hers. "We need to go. The crowd is leaving, and we don't want to be caught alone. Plus, we've a police report to file."

21

M olly kissed Lance on the cheek. "Pick me up in an hour?"

"On the dot." He cupped her cheek before opening the door to her cabin.

A willowy blonde sat on the extra bunk. Her short hair slicked back from her face. Ruby lips shone against her pale skin. She speared Molly with eyes the color of a summer sky. "I'm Natasha. Your cabin mate, yes?"

It'd taken longer than Molly thought for the cruise line to replace Hilga. "I'm Molly and this is Lance."

Lance nodded, glanced around the cabin, then backed out. "See you soon."

After closing the door behind him, Molly laid her camera and bag on her bed. "Boarded in Lahaina?"

"Yes. Transfer from another ship."

Molly strained to understand Natasha's heavy Russian accent. "This one is a step up for me." She lifted a hand mirror and tucked her short hair behind her ears. "Your boyfriend is handsome."

Molly plopped beside her equipment. "He isn't exactly my boyfriend."

"A ship romance, yes?"

"No." She gave a nervous laugh. "It's … complicated."

"He doesn't work onboard. I know this. I have asked questions about you." Natasha rose, standing close to six-feet tall. "What does he do? He is more than just passenger."

"Uh…" Why the third degree? She asked questions? Molly's stomach tightened, and she glanced at her watch. "Look at the time. I'd better hustle if I'm going to be ready to hit the deck. Duty calls." Her spine tingled at the other woman's stare. Molly forced a smile and ducked into the bathroom.

She turned the faucet to the desired temperature and sat on the closed toilet lid while the water adjusted. The crazy car chase, then being grilled for an hour by the local police, left her battered. They hadn't believed her anyway. Not until Lance showed his ID. Natasha's questions were most likely innocent enough. Who doesn't want to get to know their roommate?

Molly dropped her clothes on the floor and stepped into the shower. The warm spray washed away the sweat and grime, swirling the dirt down the drain with her tension. *God, I want it over.* No more deaths. No more disappearances. Couldn't he swipe his mighty hand and make it all go away? She lifted her face to the spray.

What could she and Lance do to find out who wanted to hurt her? Pinpointing the culprit would end it all. After tomorrow, they'd be at sea for five days. Nowhere to run if the danger escalated. She closed her eyes and let the water run through her hair.

Maybe she should've visited a church while on one of the islands. Received some spiritual renewing. Life on board a ship didn't leave a lot of time for church attendance. Her Bible rested on the shelf above her bunk, waiting for her to pick it up. No excuses there. Occasionally, evenings and time off allowed some time to read. Priorities needed to be set. Maybe she could start a Bible study among the crew.

Stepping out of the shower, she wrapped a towel around her body. Peering at her reflection in the mirror, she fingered curl serum through her hair, brushed mascara through her lashes, then slicked on rose-colored lip gloss. As good as she could get.

Red tinge around the whites of her eyes and dark shadows showed her exhaustion. It'd take too much effort to hide the effects of little sleep. Molly stepped from the bathroom, pulled on a pair of navy pants and a red and white striped blouse, before clipping her badge to her waist.

An open suitcase on Natasha's bunk screamed for Molly's attention. Her gaze flicked to the unlocked door. Her blood chilled at the thought of someone sneaking in while she'd showered.

The suitcase continued to beckon, drawing Molly with sinewy fingers. She knew she shouldn't, but curiosity nagged at the corners of her mind. She stepped over and turned the lock. Despite knowing it was wrong, she bent over the bunk and rifled through the red, white, and blue clothes required of Midnight Cruise employees, undergarments which brought heat to her cheeks, and a light sweater. Beneath all of it lay a manila envelope.

Without removing it from the case, Molly unclasped the lip and slid her fingers inside to pull out a handful of photographs. Her stomach clenched. Her knees buckled. The top picture on the stack was of her, leaning over the rail of the ship, camera in hand.

Someone knocked on the door, pulling a startled squeal from her. She shoved the photos back into the envelope, closed it, then let the clothes fall back into place.

"Molly?" Natasha's clipped tone reached her ears. "Why is the door locked? Open so I do not have to dig out my pass key."

Molly swallowed past the ball of cotton in her mouth. Her hand shook as she reached for the lock. Who was her new bunkmate?

Natasha frowned as she brushed past Molly. "This is my room too. Do not lock me out."

"I was changing. Didn't want anyone to barge in on me." She turned away from the flimsy excuse. She needed to request a new room. But how? What could she tell the chief purser? That Natasha had photos of her? Would he think it worth troubling himself over? She wished for more time to look through the rest of the envelope's contents. Maybe Natasha had photos of other employees. Maybe it helped her remember who was who.

Molly shook her head. Not even she believed such a story.

*

Lance rapped on Molly's door. She burst out like Satan's hounds were on her trail and grabbed his hand. "Come on. Don't want to be late."

"Don't you need your camera?"

She dashed back in the cabin and was back at his side in seconds. "Let's go."

He lengthened his stride to keep up with her fast pace. "What's wrong?"

"I'll tell you later. When we're alone." She glanced

over her shoulder.

"We are alone."

"More alone."

"On a ship? That'll be hard to accomplish."

She ducked into an empty elevator. "This'll do." The doors closed and she hit the stop button, halting them between floors. "Natasha has a picture of me in her suitcase."

"You went through her things?" Lance ran a hand through his hair. "Does she know?"

"I don't think so. Should I be worried?" Molly gazed up at him. A crease marred the skin between her eyes. "Why would she have pictures of me?"

"It doesn't sound normal." Lance leaned against the wall. He'd have to call the mainland. See if the office could dig anything up on the woman. Maybe his contact at the FBI could find out something. "Do you know her last name?"

Molly shook her head.

"Doesn't matter. I can find out." He reached around her and hit the start button. How could he protect her if her cabin mate was a potential threat? He'd have to get the captain to listen to reason. The SVP didn't seem to have enough sense to put one foot in front of the other, much less see the potential danger.

He studied the face in front of him. The jeweled eyes, the sprinkle of freckles, the hint of a dimple. How could he keep Molly safe when evil might share her room? For the first time since he'd made his promise to her, he doubted his ability to follow through. His arms ached to gather her and jump ship. Get her as far away from whatever she'd stumbled into as possible.

"What is it?" Her eyes widened.

"Nothing." He forced a smile. "Let's get to the dining room. I'll figure out what we need to do about sleeping arrangements."

The trust in her eyes as she gave him a slow nod, tugged at his heart. *Please, God, let me be able to keep my promise.*

They stepped out of the elevator into the din and crush of passengers making their way to the dining room. Molly halted, causing him to stop short to avoid bumping into her.

"Maybe we should post the picture somewhere." She turned.

"What do you mean?"

"Obviously, the man in the photo thinks I know who he is. If it's Morrison, then I took his picture again at the lighthouse."

"Why would he care, Molly?" Lance led her to a sofa in the foyer. "If you knew who he was, you would've reported him to the police when we found Antonio's body."

She bit her lip. "Okay. Then we set a trap. Make him think I want something from him. Blackmail, maybe."

Dangerous, but it might work. Could it be possible Morrison actually did think Molly played some kind of a game? That he thought she'd found the money and taken his picture on purpose? Lance felt there was more to the story. He doubted Morrison worked alone. What, exactly, was going on aboard the *Destiny*? It had to be more than a couple of snapshots.

He spotted Natasha entering a door opposite the elevator.

Lance grabbed Molly's elbow and pulled her to her

feet. "Let's go back to your cabin."

"Passengers aren't allowed—"

"I know, but I've had a brainstorm." He left at a pace that caused Molly to jog beside him. When they reached the cabin and she unlocked the door, he motioned her inside, then closed them in.

"Sorry for the impropriety." He stood and glanced around the room. Sheets of paneling covered the walls. Removable tiles covered the ceiling. He yanked open the small closet and felt around the carpet. Nothing.

"Watch the door." Lance stood on top of Molly's bunk and popped one ceiling tile after another until he found one that didn't move easily. Bingo! "Climb up here, Molly." The mattress bounced with her weight.

The space between the ceiling and the floor above them was maybe six inches, small enough for Molly to squeeze an arm inside. "I'm going to lift you. See if you can find anything in there." Putting his hands around her waist, he lifted her with ease.

Molly tried fitting her head into the opening. Lance's legs wobbled on the mattress.

"Hold still." He wrapped his arms around her. His healing wound protested. "You won't fit through there."

"I see something." She squirmed some more. Her flailing legs caught him in the upper thigh. He sagged against the wall.

"Don't drop me!"

"Stop kicking." He braced himself by bending his knees and balancing her on his thighs.

"There's a duffel bag! No, wait, there's two!" She grunted and dragged one toward her, letting it fall at his feet. The second one followed.

Lance lowered Molly then jumped to the floor, his leg muscles screaming in protest. She grinned up at him. "Case solved."

"Not yet, sweetheart." He unzipped one of the bags. Stacks of bills filled it. He grinned at Molly. "Your taking that picture was purely coincidental. This is what Morrison is after."

She leaned closer. "The money he's embezzled! Why my cabin?"

"No idea, but we need to let Cohn know."

"Do you think he'll resolve the issue when we land in the morning?"

"I imagine so." A weight lifted off Lance's shoulders. The days at sea would be much safer for Molly. Now, to find a place to stash the money until he found Cohn.

22

Molly grunted beneath the weight of one of the bags before she hooked it comfortably over her shoulder. "Let's find Cohn. Do you know which cabin is his?"

"We can ask the purser." Lance grabbed the other stash of cash.

Before leaving the room, Molly glanced up and down the corridor. A handful of employees headed to their rooms or duty stations. Hopefully, no one would think twice about seeing a couple carrying bags. Even during the dinner hour. She almost skipped to the purser's station, relieved to finally put an end to the nightmare of the last week. Once the money was locked in the safe, she could enjoy her job and the few days left with Lance.

Ten minutes later, she listened in disbelief as Bob Dickson stood behind the counter and told them there was no Will Cohn listed on the passenger list. "That can't be." She let the bag fall at her feet. "He's an FBI agent investigating one of the passengers."

Bob glanced at the list in his hand. "Then he's registered under a different name. Maybe he's undercover."

"Then why would he come up to Officer Spencer

175

and introduce himself?" She planted her right fist on her hip and tried to look intimidating.

Lance drew her to the side. "There's something rotten at sea, Miss Molly." He ran a hand through his hair before holding up a hand when she started to speak. "Let me think."

Indignation coursed through her. "Excuse me." She crossed her arms. What was there to think about? You didn't have to be a rocket scientist to figure out Cohn wasn't who he said he was. "You're a cop. You should've known his identification was false."

"No, what I should've done was verified with the FBI. His badge looked authentic." He grabbed the bag she'd been carrying in his free hand. "Come on. We're heading to the internet room."

"Why not make a phone call?"

"Because whoever's behind what's been going on is one step ahead of us. I'm not going to chance anyone listening in. I'll send an email. We'll have some kind of answer in the morning."

She trotted to keep up with him. "But what about the money? We can't put it back in my room."

"If they come looking for it, and it's not there, somebody's going to be upset. The target on your back will get bigger."

No way. "I'm willing to take my chances. Lock it up with the purser." What if Natasha were involved? Molly couldn't trust anyone but Lance until the whole thing was over.

Natasha towered over Molly by almost a foot. If she were mixed up in things and went looking for the cash and found it missing, she'd most likely believe her partner, if she had one, had already retrieved it. Molly still hadn't accepted the fact that her roommate intended her harm. She could've gone psycho in the shower earlier if that was her intention.

Like an obedient puppy, she followed Lance to a room which housed ten computers. Lance chose the one farthest from the entrance, set the bags on the floor, then pulled out a chair. Within seconds the ticking-tacking of keyboard keys filled the otherwise silent space. Lance stuck out the tip of his tongue as he typed. Smiling, she sat in the seat next to him.

When he'd finished, he leaned back in his chair and folded his arms behind his head. "My buddy's on the computer. We'll wait a couple of minutes and see whether he gets back to us."

Molly shrugged. She obviously wasn't cut out for detective work. All the sitting around had gotten boring, then when the action started, fear set in. She'd much rather make people happy and mind her own business. A ding drew her attention back to the monitor.

"Huh." Lance leaned forward. "Dickson must be right."

"About what?"

"Cohn must've registered under an assumed name. There's a Will Cohn working for the FBI. Here's his photo. It's a couple of years old, but definitely him." Lance rubbed a hand over his chin. "All we have to do now is find him and let him know about these bags. In the meantime, we head back to Dickson and have him lock them in the safe. We'll have to take our chances that the perpetrator doesn't try to retrieve them until we reach Vancouver."

"You mean Morrison. And what about my roommate?"

"As I've said numerous times, Molly, we only suspect Morrison. We don't have any proof on him or Natasha. Do you know of any reason to request a change of cabins?"

Molly sucked her lower lip in-between her teeth. She didn't. Chances were they sailed with a full crew and there wouldn't be any bunks available.

"There's an extra bunk in my cabin."

Her face flamed just thinking about sharing a room with Lance. "No, I couldn't do that." Innocent or not, it wouldn't look right. Anymore than him sleeping in Hilga's empty bunk.

Vince might've stolen her innocence, but a girl still had to hold onto her morals. No matter how enticing the man.

Lance laughed and turned back to the screen. "I'd find somewhere else to sleep. The weight room, foyer, anything." Another blip and he squinted at the computer. "Interesting. Cohn hasn't checked into headquarters for a couple of days."

"What does that mean?"

"I'm not sure. First thing, we lock up this money. Second is dinner. I'm starved."

*

He smiled at Molly's worried expression. Anything to lessen the severity of the crease between her brows. "You go pretend to do your job. I know you won't be able to focus completely." He placed a hand on her lower back. "It'll work out, Molly. I promise."

"There you go again. Making promises you might not be able to keep."

Without looking inside the bags, Dickson took one in each hand. Lance waited until the purser locked up the money, then steered Molly into the dining room. The familiar clatter of silverware, laughter, and muted conversation mixed with the smells of beef and chicken. Lance's stomach rumbled. Some vacation. He spent the majority of it tired, hungry, or trying to keep himself and Molly from being killed.

Now, the found fortune hung over their heads. *Lord, what have I gotten myself into?* Couldn't he take R&R like any other man?

He studied Molly's heart-shaped face, amazed at how quickly his grumbling stopped. She quickly became worth anything he might go through to keep her safe. He faltered. How had his affection for her grown so quickly?

Molly stepped away from him and moved around the circumference of the room, snapping photos of posed passengers. Her smile looked forced, too wide and pasted on a too-pale face.

No sign of Cohn in the dining room. He picked Morrison out of the crowd. The man winked at the young woman he'd been spotted with at the seven pools, for once his mood seemed lightened. Not the glowering man from the beginning of the voyage.

Choosing a seat at his usual back corner table, Lance kept an eye on the door. If he could spot Cohn before he entered the room, he might be able to speak with him without Morrison knowing. He smiled as the waitress brought his dinner, then lifted his fork.

What clues did he have to suspect Morrison? Other than Cohn's investigation into embezzlement. The man's brooding personality? Not good enough. The way he seemed to be everywhere Molly was? Could be coincidence. They were on a ship after all. Not a lot of places to be alone. Cop's instinct? Lance chose to go with that idea. He speared a bite of steak. But Morrison, being the likely suspect, didn't necessarily mean he was the one responsible for the crimes.

The medium-rare beef finally made it to his mouth. Lance leaned back and savored the blackened seasoning on top. The captain nodded as he passed and Lance returned the gesture.

Had the Hawaiian police discovered anything about the body in the warehouse? Lance rose and stepped outside the room while he kept tabs on Molly's whereabouts. He pulled his cell phone from his pocket and punched in the numbers to the police.

"This is Officer Spencer. I'm checking on the possible homicide that took place in a warehouse on the dock in Honolulu."

"One moment, please." A woman's pleasant voice sang across the air waves.

"This is Detective Okymoto."

"Spencer here. Have we found out anything?" Lance watched as Molly strolled from one table to the other.

"Alberto Juarez. Small-town crook with a rap sheet a mile long. Nothing to tie him to Morrison or the ship."

Lance ran a hand through his hair. "Thanks. I'll keep in touch." He flipped his phone closed and headed back to his seat.

Having the name of a two-bit thug didn't explain why two satchels of money had been hidden in Molly's cabin. Crime-solving onboard the *Destiny* was going nowhere fast. He needed help. Like now.

Where was Agent Cohn?

23

I still say you should sleep in my cabin." Lance leaned against the wall outside Molly's room.

"No, I'll stay here. If Natasha is involved, she won't suspect that I know a thing." She put her hand on the knob. "If she says anything, I'll play dumb." That ought to be easy, considering she knew very little. "Goodnight."

Lance's gaze settled on her lips. Would he kiss her?

She licked her lips and tilted her chin.

His eyes darkened, then he straightened. The middle of a murder investigation was not the time for romance. He should've held back before now. "Goodnight. Call me if you need anything. Lock your door."

"I will." She never should have told him about Vince. Now the man acted like a skittish rabbit. She opened the door and slid inside, closed it, then leaned back and ran a finger over her lips. What she wouldn't give for a repeat of the undercover kiss on the sidewalk a few days ago.

"Late night?" Natasha barged from the bathroom and flounced on her bunk. Molly jerked as Natasha glanced toward the ceiling and crossed her arms.

"Not too late. It's only ten o'clock." Molly forced herself not to follow the other woman's glance.

Perspiration broke out on her upper lip driving away all thought of kissing Lance. "How did your first evening go?"

"Okay." Natasha folded her legs and slid beneath the covers. Her icy eyes flickered again to the ceiling above Molly's bunk.

"Is something wrong?" Molly grabbed her nightgown and paused at the bathroom door.

"No. Nothing." Natasha set her jaw firmly and rolled to face the wall.

Molly finished preparing for bed and shakily climbed beneath her own blankets.

Natasha knew. Her continuous looking at the ceiling tiles could not be Molly's imagination. She studied the ceiling. They weren't out of order. Molly wrapped her arms around her to halt her shivering.

Would Natasha kill her in her sleep? Drag her off to be questioned by Morrison? Her heart beat in her throat, thundering in her chest. Maybe she should've stayed with Lance and hanged the consequence. God would understand, right? She knew he would, considering the circumstances, but she wouldn't get any more sleep in Lance's cabin than here. In his cabin, the distraction would be definitely different, and she wasn't sure which was the more dangerous.

She kept her purse close to her side. If Natasha attacked, there wouldn't be any time to search for it and dig out her cell phone. Her eyelids grew heavy and she forced them open. Can't sleep. Not tonight.

She blinked and opened her eyes to the sight of Natasha dressing. Molly glanced at her watch. Six a.m. She'd slept and woke up alive. *Thank you, God.* Taking a deep breath, she swung her legs and stood.

Clothes peeked from her drawer. She cut a sideways glance at Natasha. She knew she'd closed the drawer last night. Fine. If her cabin mate thought she'd hide thousands of dollars in cash beneath her underwear then more power to her. "Good morning!"

Natasha grunted and left the room, slamming the door behind her. Molly couldn't hold back her giggle. Despite being terrified of being murdered in her bed, she'd fallen asleep only to awaken and find her clothes rummaged through by a very disgruntled roommate. She couldn't wait to tell Lance as they continued their tour through the island town of Lahaina. Their last port before setting sail toward Vancouver.

A knock sounded at the door. Molly opened it with a grin on her face. "Good morning."

One corner of Lance's lip curled, giving him a debonair look, despite the evidence he'd slept very little again. "Why so cheerful?"

"I'm alive." She chuckled and pulled the door closed.

"You expected not to be?" The dimple she loved winked from his cheek.

"Yes, actually." She led the way to breakfast, enjoying the warm hand at her back. In the space of a few days, she welcomed his touch. Craved it. How different from Vince this man proved to be. Still prone to anger, but able to hold it in check, Lance treated her like an equal, not an object.

He pulled out a chair for her, then chose one beside her. "You know, the fact that the money is missing from its hiding place will most likely work in your favor. They won't be sure whether you have it or not. They'll want you alive to question you."

"Oh, goody. Something to look forward to." Molly rested her chin in her hand. Her mood swung from ecstatic to melancholy in the time it took to breathe. Maybe she needed to see a psychiatrist.

Lance chuckled and laid a hand on her shoulder. "Cheer up. The cruise is almost over."

She peered at him through lowered lashes. Did that thought not bother him in the slightest? Is that all she was to him, a job? They'd spent almost every waking moment of the last week together. Fine. If that's the way he wanted things to go.

Molly clamped her lips together, shoved back her chair, stomped out of the dining room, and then stormed down the gangplank. She'd lost her appetite.

*

What's wrong with her? Lance ran a hand through his hair and moved to follow. A simple joke could send her off faster than a rogue wave out to sea. Even though his partner had been a woman, he wasn't any closer to understanding the way their mind worked.

Molly waited with crossed arms on the dock. "There's no need for a car today. I'd rather walk." Her gym shoes slapped the concrete as she practically ran away.

"Molly, wait." Lance quickened his pace and grabbed her arm.

She yanked free, but not before he saw the sheen in her eyes.

"Are you crying?" He'd rather face another bullet than her tears.

"No." Her cheeks reddened and she lifted her chin before continuing at her rapid pace.

He caught up with her again. "Please stop and tell

me what's wrong."

She whirled fast enough, he had to take a step back in order to prevent her head from connecting with his chin. "If you don't know, I'm not going to tell you. You … you … oh, you stupid man!" Molly stomped her foot and ducked into the nearest art gallery.

Stupid? Ouch! A stab right to the heart. Lance squared his shoulders and scratched his jaw. He glanced up and down the sidewalk, at a loss as to how to proceed. Should he follow her inside, or give her a few minutes alone? He decided on the latter and turned to lean against the brick outer wall. Art wasn't his forte anyway. Neither were women's emotions, obviously.

A whaling ship towered over the harbor. Lance studied its sleek lines while he waited. Would life have been any simpler in years gone by, sailing on a ship, worrying about nothing more than the day's catch?

Molly stepped from the gallery, gave him a cold look, and motioned with her head for him to follow. Like an obedient servant, he did. He occupied his time admiring her graceful curves, the way her hips swayed when she walked, and the way her curls bounced in the tropical sun.

"Are you finished ogling me?" Molly turned. "How would you like it if the tables were turned?" She let her gaze travel over him.

Lance laughed. "I wouldn't mind."

"Good grief." Her mouth twitched. "You're incorrigible."

He slipped her hand through the crook of his arm. "But you can't help but like me anyway, can you?"

"That's the problem," she muttered.

The reason for Molly's bad mood hit upside the

head like an anchor. The reason for Molly's bad mood. He couldn't have held back his grin if he tried. She cared for him and thought he didn't feel the same.

He grabbed a handful of flowers from a street vendor, thrust a twenty-dollar bill into the woman's hand, and bowed as he gave the flowers to Molly. Her cheeks turned rosy.

"They're beautiful."

"Not as beautiful as you." He wrapped an arm around her waist. "Let's grab something to eat."

"We skipped breakfast, didn't we? I'm sorry about that." She buried her face in the blossoms.

"Molly." Lance lifted her chin so she faced him. "Everything will be okay."

"You keep saying that. Yet people keep dying or disappearing."

"I'm talking about us." He drew her out of the way of strolling tourists and sat on a bench beside the ocean. He wasn't good at expressing his feelings. How could he convince her he didn't plan on taking a hike once the cruise was over?

The breeze blew strands of hair into her face. Lance reached over and tucked them behind her ear before planting a kiss on her upturned nose. "There's something about you, Molly Nicholson."

Her eyes brightened. "I'm not just a job to you?"

"How could you think that? I'm supposed to be on vacation. If I weren't drawn to you, I could've let the local police handle things."

"They aren't doing a very good job."

"They're doing the best they can." He straightened and spread his arms along the back of the bench. "But I'm talking about us."

She rose and took his hand. "Are you sure this isn't just about that steamy kiss on the bench?"

Or any of the other places. "That's most of it. I'd like to try again." He stood and lowered his head, leaning toward her.

She pushed him away and giggled. "Let's eat before we make a public spectacle of ourselves." Or she crossed over a line into public wantonness. Help her, Lord, but the man was enticing.

"Party pooper." Steps lightened, but his mind still muddled over the moodiness of women, Lance let her lead the way to a street vendor where they purchased sweet rice wrapped in Tao leaves.

He'd taken his last bite of the honey-flavored stickiness when Cohn rounded the corner. The agent's eyes widened as Lance met his gaze, then he turned and dashed back the way he'd come. Lance grabbed Molly's hand. "Come on."

24

Molly dropped the last of her rice when Lance yanked her arm. Her camera bag banged against her thigh. She slid with an awkward surfing move and let out a yelp as he dragged her with him. "Where's the fire?" Couldn't they spend time together without her being tugged? Maybe they should've stayed snuggled on the bench.

"I don't want him to get away." Their feet pounded down the sidewalk.

"Who?"

"Cohn. We need to let him know about the money we found. And I'd like to know why he's running from us."

"You said he wanted any information we could give him." Molly gasped for breath as they rounded the corner. Cohn was nowhere to be seen.

"That's my point."

She pulled her hand free of Lance's and bent over to gulp a lung full of life-saving air. Even the fresh ocean air couldn't disguise the rotten odor of spoiled food coming from the nearby dumpster. Her stomach rolled, threatening to lose the brunch she'd just eaten.

Lance punched his thigh. "What is with these people? Do we exude some kind of odor? Everyone we need to speak to avoids us like the plague. Makes me suspicious."

Molly straightened and planted fists on her hips, her breathing still labored. "You're imagining things. The SVP always listens, kind of. The captain gives you his attention, divided though it might be. He's a busy man. Cohn is an undercover agent. He needs to make sure he remains anonymous."

"In the city," Lance leaned against the side of the building and brushed an arm across his perspiring forehead, "officers know who their enemies are, who has their back, and who prefers to put them six feet under. Here," he shook his head, "I have no idea. Nothing makes sense."

If Lance couldn't make heads or tails out of their circumstances, Molly sure couldn't. But maybe, if they sat down and talked things over, something would pop up. "Let's find a table somewhere and go over what we do know. There's a coffee shop around the corner."

Once they sat at a wrought iron bistro-style table and chairs, surrounded by fragrant island blossoms that effectively erased the pungent garbage odor from her nostrils, Molly withdrew a small spiral notebook from her camera bag. "Okay. The crime is murder. Our suspect is Robert Morrison."

"And you suspect him of this, why?" Lance crossed his arms.

"Because he creeps me out." Good grief. Hadn't they established him as their primary suspect days ago?

Lance raised his eyebrows. "That's not enough of a reason."

"Then you tell me why. You're the cop. I've been following your lead on this whole thing." Molly glared at him. "I haven't a clue what I'm doing, except trying to stay alive."

"I don't know why yet. Instinct? But something doesn't mesh." He ordered two iced coffees from a passing waitress. "Plausibility? Being convicted of embezzlement would be enough reason for some people to kill."

"Most people." Molly scribbled his comments beside Morrison's name, then added Natasha as the second name. She glanced up to see Lance scowling at her. "What?"

"Would you kill someone for money?" His eyes narrowed. "Or any reason for that matter?"

The pencil fell from Molly's trembling fingers. "I … don't think so. Maybe. If my life depended on it. Or someone I cared about. Never for personal gain." Surely, he'd fired his weapon at people. Maybe killed one or two. Why give her a hard time over a simple comment?

"Okay." As if he hadn't put her on the spot, Lance continued. "Why her?" He leaned forward and pointed at Natasha's name.

"Women's intuition. She acts like she knows the money is missing." Molly picked up and pointed the pencil at him, amazed at how much she enjoyed brainstorming with him, when he wasn't making a sideways accusation of her motives. It almost made her feel like a real police officer. Not to mention drinking coffee and talking seemed like a date.

Her gaze fell on his lips. How would he respond if she initiated the kiss? Both times he had, and not for romantic reasons. Her face flamed remembering the kiss on the beach. She forced her attention back to the notepad before she made a fool of herself.

"What she doesn't know is who took it. She can't accuse me, because what if I'm not aware there was a fortune stashed above my bed? What if her partner took it? Or the cleaning crew, for some reason."

Lance gave her a crooked grin. "You're good at this."

The waitress arrived with their coffee, and Molly took a drink of caffeine heaven. "I used to watch a lot of TV."

His laugh rang across the courtyard. A few customers smiled their way. "That's not a realistic portrayal of the justice system."

She wadded up a napkin and hurled it at him. It brushed his forehead then fluttered to his lap. She should've thrown something harder. But even that would've bounced off his hard skull. "One second you're commenting on how good I am, the next you're ridiculing me. Make up your mind, Lance Spencer. Am I an idiot or not?"

"Anything but." His face darkened. "You switch moods faster than the sea during a storm, do you know that? Keeping up with you is like chasing embers from an exploding volcano, or…"

"Okay, I get it." She gritted her teeth and picked up the pencil. "Back to work. What could Morrison and Natasha have in common? An affair?"

"Not likely with the way he's keeping time with the waitress."

"It's a secret relationship. A cover so people won't be aware they know each other."

"More television? Sounds like a soap opera."

*

Lance watched in awe as Molly's eyelids fluttered faster than a hummingbird's wings. Bright spots of crimson dotted her cheeks as she slowly rose from her chair.

Lance bolted to his feet. "I'm sorry."

"Obviously, you can't take me seriously, so I'll be going back to the ship." With a flounce of her curls, she whirled and stormed away.

Why did he insist on teasing her? He'd had several glimpses of her temper hiding behind a lovely face. The more comfortable she got with him, the less timid she appeared. A sense of satisfaction filled him. In a matter of days, he'd helped her overcome the cloud her ex-fiancé had left hanging over her head. If teasing accomplished that, he'd make sure and keep it up. But first, hurt feelings needed soothed. And he didn't think flowers would suffice this time.

"Molly." He reached for her arm.

"Don't touch me." She yanked away.

"I'm only teasing you." He shoved his hands in his pockets. "It's wonderful to sit and brainstorm with someone again. And women see things differently than men. Your insight is invaluable."

"Don't patronize me."

"I'm not. Scout's honor." He held up two fingers.

Molly rolled her eyes. "The scout hand sign uses three fingers."

"Girl Scouts?"

She shook her head. "Still three fingers."

"You're full of useful information. I need you." His heart lurched. Three words said in jest shot into his heart like cupid's arrow. He did need her. Not just for brainstorming a cruise line murder, but because, suddenly, life seemed darker without the thought of her with him. He swallowed past the lump in his throat. "Seriously."

She tilted her head to peer up at him. "Then I apologize for my childish behavior. I really don't know what's gotten into me."

He did. The shackles of Vince were falling away, and he thanked God for her freedom.

"Oh, look." Molly shaded her eyes toward the ocean.

Parasailers floated overhead beneath chutes in every color of the rainbow. Miniscule vibrant specks against the azure sky. Lance's heartbeat accelerated just watching them. He knew what would put a smile back on Molly's face.

"Do you want to try?"

Her eyes narrowed. "You're afraid of heights, remember?"

Could he do it? Be suspended way above the ocean, tethered only by a cable? No. "I could sit on the boat and watch."

She wagged a finger in his face. "I know what you're doing, Mr. Spencer, and it's working. I'm not mad at you anymore."

"So does this mean you want to fly?"

She giggled. "No, that is too much for even me. But thank you for the thought."

Looping her arm in his, they strolled past excited tourists and meandering locals. The sun warmed their backs, the waves serenaded as they caressed the shore, and the air was filled with the heavenly perfume of exotic flowers. There was nowhere Lance would rather be at that moment than in paradise with Molly.

Molly laid her cheek against his arm and squeezed. "There's a soft heart under that tough cop exterior." She peered up at him. "And a pretty face."

"I never should've told you what I used to do for a living."

She giggled. "Probably not. Of course, I'm not sure I like being seen with a man prettier than me." With a slap to his shoulder, she dashed away.

The little imp. Lance gave chase, almost colliding with her when she skidded to a stop and ducked behind a fence.

"Over there. By the whaling ship." She lifted her camera and snapped a picture.

Lance lifted his head. Natasha stood with legs shoulder-width apart, arms crossed, and a red face. Clearly not happy with her companion. Lance shifted, trying to see who she'd made the target of her anger.

Morrison stepped away, turned, shouted something in return, then stormed down the sidewalk.

25

Lance knew before she opened her mouth that Molly would have something to say about seeing Morrison and Natasha together. "I told you they were involved with each other." Molly straightened and glared at him.

"I never said they weren't. Only that we shouldn't jump to conclusions." He took her hand and continued their walk to the ship.

"I have a bad feeling about this." Molly shivered. "Sometimes, I know these things. Like women's intuition."

"Really? The first time you've mentioned it."

"Don't get mouthy." She increased her pace and practically dragged him up the gangplank. "We need to stand at the railing and watch them board. See if they arrive together."

Molly Nicholson was going to give him gray hair. "If you're in danger, letting them know you're watching is not a wise thing to do."

"You're here. What could possibly happen?" She crossed her arms across the top rail. "Besides, you're still carrying a weapon, right?"

"I'm not going to shoot on a crowded ship, Molly." Lance shook his head. Yep, she definitely watched too

197

much television. He propped a leg on the bottom rail. A breeze blew the scents of seaweed and suntan lotion past him.

Passengers chatted and laughed as they trickled in small groups to board the ship. Their last day on the islands, then five days at sea. Hopefully, Lance wouldn't go stir-crazy. Of course, the woman at his side would keep things from getting boring. But that long away from land also put her more at the mercy of a killer and a thief.

He straightened. Morrison shoved his way through the group of giggling high school graduates and dashed inside. A hundred yards behind him, Natasha strolled, head held high. She paused and glanced to where he and Molly waited.

Molly gave a wave. "Might as well pretend nothing is happening."

Natasha set her lips in a firm line, and proceeded past them.

Uh-oh. Prior experience told Lance that was not a good sign. "Come on." He laid a hand on Molly's back. "Let's go in. Something's up."

"What do you think it is?" Molly's eyes widened. "They wouldn't try anything during daytime, would they?"

Lance shrugged. "No telling, but we need to make sure we're surrounded by people. No hanging over the railing or hiding out in hallways."

He led her into the grand foyer, marveling again at the beauty and size of the marble and glass staircase. Even the passengers who bought the cheapest staterooms confronted elegance around every corner. Someday, when he didn't have a woman to keep alive,

Lance intended on taking another cruise and actually having time to enjoy the trip. Even better would be a vacation taken with Molly.

Natasha approached them with Jack Morley at her side. She thrust a finger in Molly's face. "There she is. I demand compensation."

*

Molly shoved her hand aside. "Excuse me?"

"Miss Nicholson, please follow me." The SVP turned and headed toward his office. His shoes clicked across the tiled floor.

Natasha lifted her chin. Molly glared. What had the woman told security? Dread filtered down Molly's back and into her bloodstream. "Come on, Lance."

"Mr. Spencer may wait outside my office." Morley held open his door.

"I prefer he come with me." Molly squared her shoulders. "There's nothing you can say to me that he can't hear."

Once inside, Morley waved a hand toward the three extra chairs in the room. "Have a seat, please." He lowered himself into a leather office chair, then steepled his fingers. "There has been a serious accusation made against you, Miss Nicholson. By Miss Borovsky."

"I've done nothing to her." Molly clenched her hands together in her lap. The vinyl seat squawked beneath her.

"You lie." Natasha flicked a hand in her direction. "You stole from me."

"Stole what?" Molly cut a glance to Lance. He imperceptibly shook his head.

"Money. From my suitcase." The woman's glare

shot daggers into Molly's stomach.

"The only thing I saw worth mentioning in your suitcase…" Too late. Molly clamped her lips together.

"Ah, so you confess!"

"I do no such thing." Time for a new direction. "Why do you have photos?" There. Molly glanced at Morley.

"So I can identify my new roommate. Why else? Very innocent, I assure you. But you," Natasha stabbed a finger in Molly's direction, "are a thief. You admit it."

"No, I, uh, Lance?" Why did he sit there like a lump? He could help her!

Morley's sigh interrupted. "Miss Nicholson. Miss Borovsky. Until we get to the bottom of this, I'm afraid I will have to have both of you resign from your positions."

"You're firing me?" Molly fought back tears.

"No, just a minor suspension. You will continue on the cruise. By the time we reach Vancouver, I will have reached a decision." He flipped over a sheet of paper on his desk. "You two are roommates, I presume. Since you, Miss Nicholson, were in the room first, you may stay. I will move Miss Borovsky." He frowned and shuffled through a stack of papers. "You don't seem to have good luck with roommates, Miss Nicholson."

"I do not want a different cabin." Natasha crossed her arms. "Make her leave."

"That is my decision. Miss Borovsky, you are excused. Miss Nicholson, Mr. Spencer, please stay a moment."

Natasha rose and left, slamming the door behind her. Molly cringed at the bang.

"Detective, I'm assuming you chose to keep your profession a secret from Miss Borovsky. But, regardless of your relationship with Miss Nicholson, I must insist you keep her under a professional watch." Morley leaned forward and rested his elbows on his desk. "Stealing is a serious offense aboard the *Destiny*. I'm sure you understand that."

"But, I…" Molly cut off her protests when Lance raised a hand.

"Yes, sir. I agree fully."

"There's two…"

Lance kicked her under the table.

She huffed and settled back in her seat. What kind of game was he playing? Letting her be accused of a crime. She'd never been more humiliated in her life. "Wait a minute. I'm a contracted employee. You can't fire me."

Morley rolled his head on his neck. "I have already spoken to your employers. They gave you high recommendations, thus my decision to suspend, rather than terminate."

"Oh, then, thank you." Heat flooded from her neck to her face.

The SVP folded his hands and cemented his gaze on Molly. "Your friend, Antonio, was killed. Hilga has disappeared. Now, you are accused of stealing. Life aboard this ship has not been good to you, Miss Nicholson. Take care."

She shuddered and tried to brush off the cloud of fear threatening to hover over her head. "I will."

Lance stood and held out a hand. "Thank you, Mr. Morley. I'll watch out for Miss Nicholson."

"I trust you will. Good day."

Molly stifled the urge to follow Natasha's example of slamming the door behind her, instead whirling to face Lance. "Why didn't you stick up for me?"

"Lower your voice." He led her to a settee beside a potted plant and lowered her into it. "I wanted to see how things played out. Besides, you did go through her luggage and if I said anything, it would alert people to the location of the bags."

"Oh." Molly arched her eyebrows. "Well, then, how, exactly, did they play out?"

"I have no proof—yet. But I believe Natasha suspects you of taking the money." Lance sat beside her. "Morley doesn't seem to know anything about it, or he wouldn't have been so eager for me to guard you. Plus, I no longer consider him a suspect. He seemed genuinely concerned for your welfare. His request for me to stick close makes it harder for people to get to you." A muscle twitched in his jaw. "You almost gave Natasha exactly what she wanted."

"How?"

"If you would've told Morley the bags were stashed in the purser's safe, he would've asked her whether they were hers. She would've known right away where the money is."

"And you think Bob would've let Morley into the safe."

"Why not? He's the SVP of the ship."

"Do you trust him?

"I don't trust anybody on board this ship." He rose. "You should probably make sure Natasha packs only what is hers. I'll wait outside your cabin door."

They made their way in silence back to her room where Natasha threw things helter-skelter into her suitcase. She turned to glare when Molly entered, then tossed the manila envelope at her. "Here are your stinking pictures!"

"Where did you get them, Natasha?" Molly caught them in her right hand.

"From that other photographer."

Easy enough to clarify. Molly tossed the envelope on her bunk. She intended to confront Daniella as soon as possible.

"Now where is my money?"

"I have no idea, Natasha. I have nothing of yours, nor did I take anything from your suitcase." There.

"You lie. To me, to the security." Natasha slammed her suitcase closed and towered over Molly. "I will find out the truth and make you pay." She grabbed the case's handle and stomped to the door. "Mark my words, little girl."

Molly swallowed back the lump in her throat. The next five days at sea ought to be a lot of fun.

26

Molly stared at her dinner and pouted. What was she supposed to do now with five days at sea and no job? She glanced at the notice in the center of the table. Friday's formal night boasted a dance contest. Wonderful. She wasn't in the mood to dance.

Natasha glared at her from the buffet, Morrison had yet to show his face, and there'd been no sign of Cohn since his mad dash yesterday. Solving Antonio's death was going nowhere. Right along with Molly's mood. Ugh! She shoved her plate aside.

"This will be so boring." She frowned at Lance. How could he eat when everything was falling down around their feet? "Now, what do we do?"

He shoveled in a forkful of potatoes, chewed, and swallowed. "Nothing. Enjoy the cruise."

"That's it?" She slammed back in her seat, thrusting her legs in front of her.

He sighed and set his fork beside his plate. "What do you want to do?"

"Solve this thing and clear my name." She crossed her arms. "Before someone accuses me of something worse. Like murder."

"Don't exaggerate." He folded a strip of bacon in

his mouth.

"I'm not. I'm scared." Oh, these ridiculous tears. She forced them away so she wouldn't embarrass herself.

"Last night during my Bible reading," Lance wiped his mouth with his napkin, "I came across a Bible verse that's a perfect fix for you right now. 'When you lie down among the sheep, you are like the wings of a dove covered with silver, and the end of its wings with shining gold. -Psalm 68:13'. God is in control, Molly. His shroud of protection is over you."

"But sheep are peaceful animals. Unlike murderers and thieves."

"I'm not going to do anything without His guidance." Lance bent over his food. "I advise you to do the same."

"Is all police work like this? Sitting and waiting?" Molly cut into her steak and speared a bite.

"Pretty much. At least a lot of the time. You keep your eyes and ears open and react when the situation warrants."

"Ridiculous." She waved her fork at him. "You just don't want to put me in a dangerous situation."

"Yep."

"So, you'll sit back and let things continue and let someone else solve this."

"You hit the nail on the head."

"Then I'll investigate on my own."

She flinched at the clatter of his fork as he dropped it onto his plate. "Do that and I will advise Morley to lock you under guard and key."

"I dare you." She leaned across the table and speared him with the sternest look she could muster, straightening when another couple joined them at the table. By the look on Lance's face, the conversation was far from over.

He tossed his napkin on the table and rose. "Care for a stroll, my dear?"

"Certainly, *darling*."

In silence they rode the elevator to the upper deck. The stars seemed brighter, less dwarfed by the ship's lights. Completely a waste of a romantic evening.

Lance pulled her into a dark corner and pinned her against the wall. "You will listen to me on this, Molly, or so help me—"

She lifted her chin. "What? Beat me? Lock me up?" Her accusation was unfair and she knew it, but she'd had enough of his bossiness.

"You know me better than that." He released her and gripped his hair, making it stand on end.

She smiled at the little boy image.

"You're driving me nuts!" He sagged against the wall. "Look, Molly. You came from an abusive relationship. I sympathize, really. But don't go to the extreme in your healing process."

"What do you mean?" Her smile faded faster than a shooting star.

"Don't go from being a doormat to being a witch."

Excuse me? Is that what he thought of her? She needed to change the path of things, and fast.

"I'm sorry." Her voice shook. "Do you want to sit and watch the stars?"

"Anything but this." He followed her to two empty deck chairs.

Once they sat, Molly reached for his hand and rubbed the calluses with the tips of her fingers. A working man's hands. Vince's had been smooth. They were nothing alike. She needed to acknowledge the fact and enjoy the man beside her. Maybe he was a gift from God and she refused to accept it without a fight.

Before she could talk herself out of it, she leaned over and brushed her lips against his. His eyes widened for a second, then his hand tangled in her hair and he deepened the kiss. All worry fled at the feel of his lips. At that moment, a bullet could ram into her spine and she'd die a happy woman.

*

Lance couldn't have been more surprised if Molly had told him she'd killed Antonio and thrown Hilga overboard. But, surprise quickly turned to pleasure and the air chilled when she pulled away.

"That was nice." Her whisper caressed his ear with the softness of a feather. He reached for her again and frowned when she straightened in her chair.

"Come back here."

She shook her head. "No, that wouldn't be wise."

Probably not, considering few people strolled the deck, the moon was a sliver in the inky sky, and heat infused Lance's body. He took a deep breath to steady his heart.

Lord, I've never been a womanizer, you know that. But I will definitely need your help to toe the line with Molly. The woman stirs my blood like no one else.

"I've been wanting to do that for a while." She giggled.

"Glad you acted on it." Lance grinned and folded his arms behind his head.

"Me too." Heat rose up her neck and into her cheeks. She couldn't remember ever being so daring.

"You can do it again, if you want."

"You're a flirt, did you know that?"

"Hey, you kissed me." Strands of music drifted from somewhere below them. "Do you want to sign up for the dance competition?"

"We'd have to practice."

He laughed. "We've got three nights before the contest. It'll be fun, even if we don't win."

"They'll do more than Salsa." She turned to look at him.

"I can Foxtrot, Salsa, Rhumba, and Swing. Whatever you can throw at me. My dad hated the stuff so I was left to cut a rug with my mom." It was one of his favorite memories. She'd put on a favorite oldie and grab his hand. He missed them.

"Okay, let's do it!" She leaped to her feet. "That's a waltz they're playing. We can start practicing now."

He rose and took her in his arms, loving the way her head tucked into his shoulder. Like they'd been made to fit together. It'd be hard to hold her at arm's length in order to effectively do the steps, but twirl her he did. She was light on her feet, as if they didn't touch the wood beneath them. After the waltz, he pulled her into a Foxtrot and headed around the perimeter of the deck.

"Look." Molly stopped and pointed to a falling star. "Make a wish."

He wished the night would never end and that violence and evil would stay away, and that he could hold Molly in his arms forever.

"What did you wish for?" Her eyes glistened as she peered up at him.

"Nope. Wouldn't come true if I told you." He stared down into her upturned face and ached to kiss her

CYNTHIA HICKEY

again.

"Silly superstition." She leaned into him.

The breeze carried a whiff of the flower fragrance Lance loved. The scent that screamed Molly Nicholson. They moved to the railing and stared at the waves churned into motion by the ship.

"There isn't anything more beautiful than the ocean at night, is there?" Molly leaned her back against Lance. He braced his arms on each side of her, gripping the rail, for balance as much as to keep his hands occupied and out of trouble.

"I can think of one thing." He lowered his head to nuzzle her neck.

"Oh, no, you don't, Mr. Spencer. That's too much—"

A shot rang out and a cry for help drew their attention downward. Agent Cohn hung from the second deck, his legs flailing the air above the dark sea.

"Hold on!" Lance cast around for a life preserver.

"He's going to fall. There's no way we'll make it in time. He's two decks below us!" Molly grabbed his arm. "Your cell phone! Call the captain."

He pulled it from his pocket as Molly whirled back to peer over the edge. Her shoulder knocked his hand. The phone flew over the edge, despite Lance's lunge for it.

Cohn glanced up, reached an arm in their direction, and disappeared.

27

L ance's phone traveled the path of Agent Cohn. The silver rectangle sparkled in the ship's lights before sinking into fathomlessness. Molly's legs gave out beneath her. She stared in disbelief. How could this happen?

Lance groaned, slapped the top rail, and then dashed inside. He poked his head out the door. "Come on!"

After pushing to her feet, Molly whirled, then followed and struggled to keep up with his long-legged sprint. Lance skidded to a halt next to a courtesy phone, punched in directory, then barked out directions to the Lido deck about a man overboard.

Molly fought back tears. She'd heard what sounded like a gunshot. No way could she convince herself Cohn fell over on accident. Someone helped.

Lance hung up the phone. He grabbed her hand, a gesture quickly becoming way too commonplace for them, and dragged her after him. They made a beeline to where Cohn disappeared.

"I can't see him." Lance leaned so far over the railing Molly thought he'd fall. When someone was in danger, there was no sign of his phobia. Under different circumstances, the thought would've made her smile.

The water churned beneath them with waves of

cream and ink. "I don't either."

Feet pounded behind them, and Molly spun as Jack Morley and several other security personnel stampeded toward them. Morley's expression was as dark as the sea.

"Miss Nicholson again. Misfortune seems to follow you."

"Not by choice." She crossed her arms.

Lance stepped forward. "Molly isn't the issue here. From the top deck, we saw a passenger go overboard. It's the FBI agent that is supposedly not listed as a passenger."

Morley looked taken aback. "I wasn't aware we had the FBI onboard."

"He was investigating a passenger undercover." Lance flung his arms wide. "And he's gone overboard! It doesn't matter who he is! Why are we standing around debating this?"

Morley motioned for his men to move. "Follow procedure."

Like that helped Hilga. Molly slid down the closest wall and squatted on the deck, putting her head in her hands. Without the FBI onboard, she and Lance would be on their own.

"We can't do anything here." Lance held out a hand to pull her to her feet. "I need to contact my friend in the bureau. Let him know about Cohn."

Once in the internet room, Lance sent an email to his contact then leaned back in his chair. A frown marred his brow. He sighed and rubbed his temples. "I need some sleep."

"I can lock myself in my cabin." Molly glanced at her watch. "It's only ten o'clock. We could both use a good night's rest." She doubted she'd sleep, but the idea definitely had merit.

"Waiting for a response to my email seems more responsible."

She laid a hand on his shoulder. "You won't be good for either one of us if you collapse from exhaustion."

"You're right." He cupped her hand. "An answer will still be there in the morning."

Like a couple well past their golden years, they made their way to Molly's room. Lance placed a tender kiss on her lips, took the pass card from her hand, and opened the door. After a quick run through the room, he deemed it safe for her to enter.

"Goodnight, Molly. Keep your cell phone close."

"I will." After he disappeared around the corner, she closed the door and leaned against it. They'd shared a kiss that would set the ship on fire, then another body went overboard. Her life resembled a roller-coaster. All she lacked was the upside-down loop. She had no doubt it would come.

Her steps dragged as she went into the bathroom and shed her clothes. Sitting on the lid of the toilet, she waited for the shower to adjust to a comfortable temperature. The tile behind her cooled her heated back and kept her from falling asleep where she sat.

Lord, I'm tired. Not just physically, but mentally too. Please help us out of this mess before more people die. I'm sorry I thought Lance and I would be alone with Cohn gone. You'd never forsake us. Thank You.

She tested the water, deemed it hot enough to wash away the day's stress, then stepped beneath the shower's cleansing flow. The temptation to withdraw the money from the purser's safe slammed into her. If she handed the money back to Morrison, maybe it would all stop. And maybe he'd shoot her on the spot, taking out a witness.

Her next breath caught in her throat. Hyperventilation threatened, and Molly slid to the floor of the stall. Who was she kidding? She wasn't strong enough for this. Why did she entertain the idea she was? She should've fled in Maui and got the next plane back to the States where she could've disappeared in the millions of faces on the mainland.

Staying here trying to solve the case would only get her and Lance killed. The thought stole her next breath, catching on the giant sobs that ripped through her.

Buck up, Molly. She forced herself to her feet. Whether she wanted it or not, danger had thrust itself into her life. Crying wouldn't make it go away. She finished her shower, donned her nightclothes, and climbed beneath the cool sheet on her bed. Reaching for her phone, she dialed Lance's room number.

*

As tired as he was, Lance headed back to the deck to see how the search for Cohn went. Morley met him halfway.

"Nothing, detective. Not a scrap of fabric, a shoe, nothing." Morley rubbed his face. "This has been the cruise to beat all, and somehow, Miss Nicholson is in the middle of it. If you know why, I'd like in on the information."

Lance took a deep breath and let it out slowly. "Cohn was investigating the passenger Robert Morrison—"

"I know that man. Overextended his credit card.

Had to transfer money."

Lance nodded. "He was being investigated for embezzling from the company he worked for. Molly and I found two duffel bags of cash stashed in the ceiling of her cabin. We gave the money to the purser to put in his safe. Kind of coincidental that Morrison would be short of money, yet we find a bundle hidden away."

"Does the purser know there's money in the bags?"

"I didn't tell him. Just asked him to lock them up. He might've looked."

Morley shook his head. "Knowing you're a police officer, I don't think Dickson would have peeked. No matter how tempted he was."

"I hope not. If he did, there could be a target on his back as well."

"I need to call the FBI and have them meet us in Vancouver. Nobody's going anywhere for a few days." Morley marched away, leaving Lance to watch as security personnel re-boarded the ship. Minus Cohn.

He tried rolling the tension from his shoulders as he headed to his room. At almost midnight, he'd be lucky to get six hours sleep. Molly was right. He'd be no good to anyone without rest.

Upon entering his cabin, he stopped short. His clothes and belongings were strewn from the closet and dresser. A peek into the bathroom showed his toiletries tossed in the toilet. Rage welled in him so intense he buried his fingernails into the palms of his hands. Thank the Lord he'd had his weapon with him.

After checking to see whether anything was missing, he cleared the bed and plopped onto the bare mattress. As a cop, he'd seen a lot of vandalism, but never experienced it for himself. Since the money had been hidden in Molly's room, it was clear the rifling of his served as a warning.

Stupid crooks. To an officer of the law, they'd only issued an invitation for him to continue.

Despite the lure of sleep, Lance dug his cell phone from his pocket and dialed security. "Morley, please." He was glad he'd bought a pay-as-you-go phone that morning.

"This is Morley."

"Officer Spencer, here. Someone ransacked my room." Lance laid an arm across his face to cover his eyes. No way was he getting up to turn off the light.

"So, it's a crew member. Or at least someone who knows a crew member willing to let them into a passenger's cabin."

"It would seem so." Lying horizontal was almost the best thing he'd felt all day. Outside of Molly's kiss.

"Do you want me to send someone?"

"No. I'm exhausted. Just file the report and have someone tape off the room. They can investigate in the morning." He flipped the phone closed and let it fall beside him. Shifting his weight, he pulled his weapon from his waistband and left it in easy reach of his right hand.

The jingle of his bedside phone, startled him and he reached for his gun. He grinned at his touchiness and hit the speaker button. "Hello?"

"It's me. Molly."

As if he wouldn't recognize her voice. "Are you okay?"

"I didn't wake you, did I?" The raspiness of her words told him she was close to sleep herself.

"No, not yet. What's up?"

"Did they find anything? I know you probably didn't go straight to your room."

He chuckled. "You're correct. Unfortunately, there's no sign of Cohn or foul play. But someone did tear up my room pretty good."

She gasped. "Are you all right?"

"Yeah, I'm fine. I wasn't here. Nothing's missing. It's just a warning."

"It could be anyone, Lance. Morrison shouldn't have access to pass keys."

"Someone's helping him. If he's our suspect."

"You sure don't like to admit the obvious, do you?"

"I suspect him, just don't want to say for sure until we have more evidence." He grabbed a shoe from the floor and tossed it at the light switch. Bingo! The room plunged into darkness.

"What was that?"

"Turning off the light."

"Okay." She paused. "Thank you, Lance. For helping me. I bet you didn't expect your vacation flirtation to end up like this."

"You're welcome, gorgeous. And no, but you sure keep things interesting."

28

Molly woke the next morning refreshed and smiling from falling asleep after talking to Lance. She could get used to his voice being the last thing she heard each night.

She pulled a sundress from the closet. No sense in dressing in Midnight Cruise Line's uniform if she wasn't working for them. Out of habit, she reached for her camera. No need. Without it, she wouldn't be at risk of capturing the killer's photo. No, it'd be safer to leave it behind.

But where? Not in plain sight. If someone broke into Lance's stateroom, the possibility of them entering to steal the Nikon was greater than she wanted to risk. She glanced up and smiled. She'd stash it where they'd found the money.

Camera hidden, she headed to finish getting ready, grateful for the opportunity to dress feminine. With a touch of light makeup, and her curls fluffed around her face, she was ready when Lance knocked.

"Good morning," she sang.

"You look pretty. All girly too." He reached behind her and pulled the door closed.

He seemed rested. The circles beneath his eyes had faded. In his tan carpenter shorts and black tee shirt, he looked like a California guy headed to the beach. She looked down. Yep, complete with sandals. "And you're casual, too." And looking mighty fine.

"Buffet or sit down breakfast?" Lance cocked his head.

"I haven't done the sit down on the ship. Let's try that." Molly slipped her hand into Lance's. They were like a dating couple. The end of the cruise would leave a huge hole in her life. Hopefully, she'd get her job back to help fill the void.

Lance wanted to pursue a long distance relationship, and she'd promised to try and make it work, but there was a long way between the mainland and ships at sea. With Lance's good looks, she didn't hold much hope that he'd be waiting long. Once he healed from losing his partner, he'd realize the foolishness in what he thought could work, and some gorgeous woman would get her hooks in him.

She shook off the thought. She still had a few days left with him. Anything could happen in that time.

The formal dining room was less busy and much quieter than the buffet. The soft chink of silverware against china and the low murmurs of conversation added to the ambiance.

The other photographer, Daniella, nodded as Molly and Lance entered, then returned to her job. Molly shrugged. What could the other woman do? Convince the SVP to give the job back? Chances were, the other crewmembers weren't aware of the circumstances around Molly's dismissal.

Lance held a chair out for her then sat in one beside her. "What would you like to do after breakfast? A stroll around the deck? I don't gamble, but we could visit the casino if you wanted. There's also a pottery class, I think." He lifted the menu. "There's a variety show this evening, and we could practice our dancing after that."

She twirled her water glass. Besides swimming and shuffleboard, the gym or spa, there wasn't a lot to do during the day except wander the ship. "A stroll sounds fine." Molly lifted her gaze to him. "Won't you get bored on the ship for five days?"

"Not with you." He gave her a lopsided grin. "What better way to get to know you without any distractions?"

"True." She pointed at him. "But you'll have to play along. I won't talk only about myself."

"Fair enough."

The waitress arrived, poured coffee in Lance's upturned mug and asked for their orders. Molly ordered strawberry crepes. Lance asked for a three egg omelet and bacon. At Molly's questioning look, he answered, "I'm on vacation."

"I didn't say anything." She spread her napkin in her lap. "Did you hear back from the FBI?"

"Yep. I checked before getting you." Lance took a sip of his hot coffee. "Cohn had no family. Parents dead. No siblings. He's a desk jockey given his first opportunity to prove himself. All he needed to do was keep an eye on Morrison. Not to come into contact with the man. The bureau will have a couple of agents waiting when we dock in Vancouver."

"Anything can happen between now and then."

"It can, but the perpetrator has nowhere to go except overboard."

She supposed that thought should make her feel

better, but it didn't. Instead it increased her anxiety. They were all stuck in the middle of the ocean. Together.

The food arrived. Molly tried to enjoy the cream filled pastries covered with strawberries, but they tasted like dust in her mouth. Lance dug into his like a starving man.

"Why aren't you eating?" He frowned.

"I can't." She shoved her plate away and straightened. While she waited for Lance to finish, she drank her juice and glanced around the room.

Most of the diners she'd photographed at one time or another. Her heart ached to think she'd have to spend the next few days not contributing to these people's cruise experience. Why couldn't she enjoy the gift she'd been given? The opportunity to be a tourist?

"Okay, let's walk." Lance rose and held out his hand.

She accepted and allowed him to pull her outside. Clouds covered the sky and a light mist began to fall. "Guess we'll have to find seats beneath an awning."

"This is a nice change," Lance said. "The sun doesn't have to shine every day."

It didn't, did it? Lance's presence was a ray of sunshine in itself. She'd enjoy it while she could and take cover when it disappeared.

*

After they'd chosen chairs at a table on a covered patio, Lance folded his hands and leaned forward. "Okay, now we play my version of twenty questions."

Molly raised her eyebrows. "Should I be nervous?"

"No, they're easy. First one ... what's your full name?"

"Molly Margaret Nicholson."

"Land of heritage?"

"My father was English, my mom, Irish." She cocked her head. "What's your full name?"

"Lance Michael Spencer. I'm an Italian and Cherokee mix." A waitress strolled by and Lance raised his hand to attract her attention. When she made her way to their table, he ordered two sodas. A regular for him and a diet for Molly. "Okay, what did you want to be when you grew up?"

"An artist. Photography is close. You?"

"A policeman." He chuckled. "Well, when I was five, I wanted to be a dinosaur."

The giggle he loved erupted from Molly's throat. "At least I stuck with something human. That young, I wanted to be a ballerina."

As they played, the haunted look began to disappear from Molly's face and Lance's heart lightened. "What was one thing you asked Santa for and didn't get?"

She put a finger to her lips. "Hmm. Well, my parents were fairly well-off, so I got most things I asked for. I guess, I'd say a pony."

"Mine was a rocket ship. Not a toy. A real one."

"You're not hard to please, are you?" She accepted her drink from the returning waitress, and stiffened at something she saw over his shoulder.

Lance turned. Morrison leaned against the railing, oblivious to the rain, and flicked a cigarette butt into the sea. Lance returned his attention to Molly. "Stay focused. He's not doing anything. How old were you when you got your first kiss?"

"First grade." A flush rose to her cheeks. "I had to stay after school for talking in class and the little boy who had to stay too, kissed me behind the overhead projector screen."

He wiggled his eyebrows. "Wanton. I was three. A neighbor girl."

"A regular Don Juan."

"I like to think so."

Molly's eyes widened. "Natasha just walked by. I think she handed something to Morrison, but handed it over so fast, I'm not sure. Uh-oh."

"What?"

"He's coming this way. No, wait, he's going to the other side of the pool."

"Stop staring." Lance reached across the table and turned her head back to face him. "If he does something interesting, feel free to let me know. Otherwise, I'm trying to get to know you."

"Sorry." She pursed her lips around her straw. Lance lost his focus and swallowed too much soda, sending himself into a choking fit.

Face red and eyes streaming, he gained control and fought to keep his attention off her mouth. "Uh, what would be your perfect vacation?"

"Maui. Visiting all the secret places that only the locals know about."

His stomach fluttered as nerves sent barbs into his gut. "Would that include a man?"

Her eyes darkened. "It might."

"That's—"

"She did give him something!" Molly slammed her glass on the table. "He's reading a slip of paper. Oh, now he's walking away." She rose. "Let's follow him."

They waited until he turned a corner out of sight, then followed, always keeping a few yards between them and him. Morrison ducked into a men's restroom.

"Guess I'll have to go it alone." He speared Molly with a glance. "Under no circumstances do you leave. Understood?"

She gave him a salute. "Yes, sir!"

He shook his head and pushed open the door. Morrison's gym shoe covered feet showed beneath a stall. Lance approached the mirror and pretended to examine his teeth, not turning when Morrison approached from behind.

The man went to the sink. "Still keeping time with the pretty photographer, I see."

"Helps pass the time." Through the mirror, he met Morrison's unsmiling face.

"I've heard danger goes where she does. Most of her friends among the crew have disappeared."

Lance turned. "And where did you hear that?"

"Around." Morrison gave him a thin-lipped smile. "I'd be careful if I were you."

29

Molly studied her fingernails while she waited for Lance to emerge from the bathroom. What was he doing in there? She'd never been good at waiting. Now that she seemed to spend her life on pins and needles, it was even worse. How would she ever handle a long distance relationship? Waiting for the phone to ring or for whatever ship she hired on to dock so she could spend time with Lance? She sighed. It'd never work.

Morrison barged from the room, bumping her shoulder on the way out. "Out of my way, little girl." He stormed across the foyer and outside.

Lance rejoined Molly. "Don't worry about him. He's full of threats today."

"What happened in there?"

"Not much, but it seems like the man is definitely searching for something."

"He knows we have the money." Molly's throat seized.

"Maybe, and he's trying to find out where it is. Right along with the Russian Princess." He motioned his head to where Natasha came out of the women's restroom.

"Why is that woman always around?" Molly

shivered at Natasha's stare.

"Go to the bathroom. See if she follows you back in." Lance nudged her.

"Have you seen the size of her? She's six feet tall!"

"I'll be right out here."

"Fine." Molly shrugged and shoved her way through the door. When someone entered behind her, she ducked into a stall.

"I know you are there. Come out."

"I'm busy here."

"You are procrastinating." Natasha pounded, shaking the line of stalls. "Come out and face me."

Molly closed her eyes and leaned against the wall. She might as well get this over with. With a deep breath, she stepped out. "What?"

"I want my money." Natasha crossed her arms and towered over Molly.

"I don't know what you're talking about."

"You do." Natasha poked a finger in Molly's chest. "You have it. I need it. You don't know who you are messing with."

Molly slapped her hand away. "Don't touch me."

Natasha gave her a two-hand shove that sent Molly reeling into the wall. "I will do more than that if you do not give me back what is mine."

Molly scowled. "I don't have it!" She lifted her chin. "Touch me again." No one laid an angry hand on Molly Nicholson. Not anymore.

"And what will a little woman like you do?" Natasha laughed. "Hit me? Call the bulldog waiting outside? Americans are weak people. No match for me."

Molly spread her legs shoulder-width apart and

tilted her head. "Try me." Her cousins had been Natasha's size or larger. With the few pointers Lance gave her, she could take the blond Amazon. She might get some bruises, but she'd leave plenty marks of her own.

Natasha laid the tip of her index finger on Molly's forehead. "I am touching you."

With her head lowered, Molly rammed into Natasha, slamming them both into the line of sinks against the opposite wall. The breath whooshed from Natasha before she forced Molly back. A raised knee knocked the air from Molly's lungs.

"There. See." Natasha turned, giving Molly the opportunity she needed.

With a primal yell, she launched herself onto the other woman's neck and grabbed two fistfuls of hair.

"Ow!" Natasha whirled and lost her footing.

Molly reached for the faucet, plastered her hand against the water and sprayed Natasha's face. Natasha reached over her head to try and dislodge Molly. They spun in circles so many times, Molly felt as if they were in a washing machine.

"I will kill you for this!" Natasha's shriek bounced off the tile walls.

"You'll have to catch me first!" Molly yanked back on the woman's head.

Natasha's feet slipped in a puddle of water. They crashed through the door and landed at the feet of an astounded Bob Dickson.

"Ladies! What is the meaning of this?" He grabbed Molly's arm and yanked her off Natasha.

Lance coughed and pulled Molly to him. She curved her fingers into claws and hissed at her former

CYNTHIA HICKEY

roommate before turning to him.

She glared. "Where were you? And don't try telling me that cough isn't you trying to camouflage a laugh."

"You handled yourself well enough."

She planted fists on her hips. "What were you doing? Watching through the door?"

"Yes." His eyes twinkled as he tried to keep a straight face.

"Oh, good grief." She turned back to the stern look of the purser.

"Miss Nicholson. I'm aware that you have been relieved of your duties onboard the *Destiny*, but that does not give you the right to attack the other crew members."

"She started it!" Molly took a step forward, claws ready. Lance held her back.

"I am afraid for my life." Tears welled in Natasha's eyes as she clasped folded hands over her chest. "She is out to kill me for accusing her of stealing. I know this is true."

"She's lying." Molly shook off Lance's hand. Could anyone in their right mind believe such dramatics?

"Miss Nicholson." Dickson drew himself to his full height. "I must implore that you stay away from Miss Borovsky. If I hear you approached her again, I will have you confined to your cabin."

"Of all the stupid, lame-brained—"

"Come on, Molly." Lance took possession of her arm again and pulled her along with him.

Once they were out of sight of the purser and Natasha, Lance burst into laughter. "You were like a badger. All over that woman. I thought I was going to have to douse you with cold water."

"Yeah, you should've taken pictures. Or charged admission. It's your fault." She plopped into the first deck chair she spotted and bent to examine the rug burns on her knees. "My mother would've been mortified to see me fighting. And in a dress, no less." She straightened. "What did you hope to accomplish from all that?"

He perched at the foot of the chaise. "Did she tell you anything?"

Molly tried smoothing her hair. "She wants the money and said I didn't know who I was dealing with. She might've thrown in a 'I will kill you' somewhere."

"She's scared." Lance used the end of his tee shirt to wipe a trickle of blood from her knee before bending and blowing a cooling breath across the scrape.

Molly's heart tried to beat its way through her ribcage.

*

Why did he blow on Molly's knee? The simple gesture ripped through his gut. He shouldn't have sent her to meet with Natasha alone. What did it accomplish, but more speculations?

Molly pulled the skirt of her dress down to cover her knees and heat flooded Lance's neck. He'd become too comfortable with her; too familiar in such a short time. Fear over her vulnerability after the failed romance with Vince nagged at him. Maybe neither of them was ready for something serious. Convincing his heart would be another story. It already belonged to Molly Nicholson.

"Are you okay, except for the skinned knees?"

She shrugged. "She slammed me up against the wall pretty good, but I'm tougher than I look." A grin split her face. "It was childish actually. I told her not to touch me again, and she put a finger on my head. I lost it."

Lance laughed hard enough to bring tears to his eyes. "I consider myself fair warned about your temper. I didn't know what to think when the two of you landed at Dickson's feet, and you riding piggyback on Natasha."

Molly snorted. "I didn't think. Just reacted."

Lance cupped her cheek and moved to the lounge beside her. They needed to plot their next move. "I'm sorry about asking you to do that. I'm beginning to suspect that neither Morrison nor Natasha are the brains behind this operation."

Molly paled. "There's someone else?"

"Maybe." An unknown mastermind who knew who they were, and they didn't have a clue as to his or her identity. Not a pleasant thought.

"What do we do?"

"I'm trying to figure out a way to let them know for sure that we have the money. Unless they force the purser to open the safe, we're the only way in."

Molly nodded. "Bob would never cave. He's very big on ethics."

"I agree." Lance folded his arms behind his head, pleased that his wound pulled only slightly. "Morrison would have to force us to take the money out."

"I don't like the sound of that." Molly wrapped her arms around her bent knees. "Why can't we wait until Vancouver and let the FBI handle things?"

"We could." But he didn't think things would wait that long. Gut instinct told him things were coming to a boil. And Molly was smack dab in the crosshairs. "Is that what you want?"

"I don't like sitting back and waiting, but I don't see any other option."

"Well, unless I can come up with a better plan, that's what we'll have to do. Don't let Natasha intimidate you though. A woman her size is used to using that to her advantage."

Molly squared her shoulders. "I'm not afraid of her."

"Good." She'd need that kind of spunk if they came for her.

30

I need to go shopping." Molly glanced in the window of one of the ship's boutique shops. A formal gown was out of her budget, but looking good for the evening's ballroom dance contest won hands down.

For the last two days, they'd done nothing more than practice their moves and try to keep tabs on Natasha and Morrison as they strolled the deck of the ship. The two were rarely together, but when they were, Molly did everything she could to snap their picture. An evening of glitz and glamour was exactly what she needed.

"I'm wearing my two-hundred dollar-dollar tux." Lance plopped himself down on a cushioned bench outside the door. "You go ahead. I've got a couple calls to make."

"Thanks." Molly pushed open the glass and brass doors, slipping inside a shop filled with everything a woman could want to wear onboard the ship, or off. Several women prowled the store. What if everything was picked over and she couldn't find something suitable? She couldn't wear her semi-formal black dress. Not for this evening.

Soft music provided a soothing ambiance. Women

flitted from rack to rack fingering everything from lingerie to evening gowns. Molly inhaled, breathing deep of a floral perfume. She could spend hours in here.

Instead, she strolled toward a rack of gowns. A royal blue, gauzy creation immediately attracted her attention. She glanced at the tag. Size four. Perfect. She gulped at the three hundred dollar price tag.

Too bad. She'd try it on anyway. It wasn't every day a girl got to dance with a handsome man and look like a princess. She practically skipped to the dressing room.

The dress flowed over her curves like it'd been sewn just for her. She smoothed her hands over the soft fabric. She felt beautiful wearing it.

Molly twirled in the three-way mirror and admired the way it flared around her ankles. Plenty of room to dance. She prayed the store would have shoes to match.

"May I hold that for you?" A pretty sales girl approached Molly with a smile on her face.

"Please." She handed it over. "Shoes?"

"Back right hand corner. There are a pair of silver rhinestone ones that would look lovely with this gown."

"Thank you." Molly rushed to the back. There! Sparkling beneath the fluorescent lights was a size six. It couldn't get any better.

When she exited the store, Molly was poorer by three hundred and seventy-five dollars, but immeasurably richer in the rare pleasurable instance of splurging on herself.

Lance sat where she'd left him, staring at his phone. Her steps faltered at the glowering look on his face.

"What's wrong?" She draped the bag over her arm and sat beside him.

"My contact at the bureau told me Cohn's been under suspicion for the last couple of weeks. It was all kept hush-hush. Until my email." A muscle ticked in his jaw. "That set them to doing a bit of searching."

"But he went overboard. That's good, right?"

"Depends on how you look at it." Lance rose and paced. "If he was involved in what's going on aboard the *Destiny*, then it could mean someone is getting nervous. The natives are turning on each other."

"Better them than us." The good mood from shopping evaporated like the morning mist she'd seen every morning around the Hawaiian Islands. Molly immediately felt chastised. God wouldn't want her to wish ill luck on anyone.

"Antsy people do desperate things."

*

Lance needed some definite information on Morrison to take to the SVP so the man could be locked up. If Morrison wasn't the perp, then he needed to know who was.

He hated being confined to something as small as a ship. No matter how large the vessel. On land, he would have had the resources he needed. Relying on others to locate information took too long.

The longer Morrison, or the unsub, roamed the ship, the greater the danger to Molly. Lance's heart stuttered as her face paled. He dug his fingernails into his palms to control the anger rolling through him. What if he couldn't keep her safe?

He should never have fallen for her. Things should've been left on a professional basis. Bodyguard and victim. He could've enjoyed her company. He didn't have to fall in love. Who was he kidding? The way he felt about her had nothing to do with the situation they found themselves in.

He rose and held out his hand. "I'm sorry for ruining the day."

Her smile shook. "You didn't. I've got to keep myself grounded in reality." Her shoulders slumped. "Nothing in my life is going as planned."

"Let's walk." Lance took the garment bag and a shoe box. "Right after I have the store hold these for us." He ducked into the store, handed the items to the woman behind the counter, then rejoined Molly, pulling her to her feet.

Once outside, he led her to the railing. "You were happy when you went into the store, what happened?"

"Your phone call is what happened." Molly leaned her back against the rail and hooked her arms through. "I'm thirty and not engaged, nor do I have any prospects. I took what I thought was my dream job and it's turned into a nightmare. Now, I don't even have the job. I have no friends on board, because everyone seems to want to kill me. Are you getting the picture?"

Lance released his breath in a way that puffed out his cheeks. He should've waited until he dropped her off in her cabin before calling his source at the station. Since they'd shared all other aspects of the drama surrounding her, he hadn't thought. Instead, he'd ruined what promised to be a wonderful evening and had no idea how to make it up to her.

"Life happens. And most of the time not in the way we figured." Lance propped a foot on the bottom rail. "From what I've learned, God has a plan. We don't always know what it is, but we can rest assured that He's in control." He glanced at her. "That doesn't mean man doesn't have free will, but we need to trust that God will see us through this."

She closed her eyes and lifted her face to the ocean breeze. "You're right. But it doesn't make things easier. I'm trying to make sense of it all," She opened her eyes and waved an arm. "And failing miserably."

He tweaked her nose. "I think you've done great. Most women would be a quivering hysterical mess in a corner somewhere."

She shrugged. "I'm more of a fall apart when it's over kind of person."

The sun began its gentle descent over the horizon, tipping the waves with crimson and gold. Lance peeked at his watch. "We need to get changed. The contest starts in an hour."

*

Molly stepped into Lance's curved arm as if she were going home, and placed her hand in his.

"You're beautiful," he whispered.

"Thank you." She counted to ten in order to control her breathing. They'd been practicing for two days. Why was she so nervous? Her gaze roamed the room. Maybe because there were several other couples on the floor and countless faces watched from the sidelines. Relax. They could do this. Lance danced like a dream.

The band struck up a swing tune and Lance pushed Molly into a triple-step then a rock step. Before she knew it, her face hurt from grinning. She'd never had so much fun. The music swelled to a waltz, then into a Foxtrot promenade around the floor. After an hour, only three other couples were left. The three judges had administered the dreaded shoulder tap to the others.

"You holding up okay?" Lance smiled down at her

during their five minute break.

"I'm having a blast. We make a good team." She sipped from her glass of ice water.

His eyes darkened. "Yes, we do."

The look on his face and three little words stole Molly's breath faster than the dancing. Her face heated and she lay the cool glass against her forehead. When Lance blew softly in her face, she'd thought she'd swoon.

"Dancers ready!" The announcer's voice cut through her thoughts as effectively as a sailboat through the water.

Lance swung her back into his arms and did a slow-quick-quick as a Salsa tune played. The music, the ambiance, his moves, were all hotter than a summer day in the desert. Oh, be still her heart.

After the dance, Molly and Lance stood in the center of the floor, his arm around her, sweat pouring down their faces, and laughs bursting from their throats as they held the first place trophy high above their heads. Even the sight of Natasha glaring at them as she distributed drinks couldn't dispel Molly's happiness.

Lance lifted Molly off the floor and twirled her, just like she'd seen the honeymoon couple do on the cruise's first day. She swallowed past the Titanic-sized lump in her throat and focused on his eyes as he set her on her feet and lowered his mouth to hers. Tears stung the back of her lids as she returned his kiss. Two more days and he'd be back on land. Whatever would she do?

Applauding exploded around them as Lance raised his head, then led her to a waiting table. He shrugged out of his jacket, untied his tie, and loosened the top buttons on his shirt. "That was the most fun I've had in a very long time. Thank you, Molly." He slid into the seat beside her.

She fanned her face with a napkin from the table. "You are a wonderful dancer."

"Only as good as my partner." He lifted his glass and downed the water.

"I can't remember ever being this tired." Molly fanned faster. "But I'd do it again in a heartbeat."

"Definitely." He rose. "Let's get you back to your room, and I need a shower."

"You're right, but I hate for the night to end." Molly slipped her arm through his and laid her head on his shoulder.

"Let's go dancing again when we hit Vancouver. I'm sure there's somewhere we can go."

"Really? You don't have to get back to work right away?"

His dimple winked. "I've got another week before I report back. There's no one I'd rather spend it with, than you."

There's no way she'd be able to sleep. Not with the way her heart raced. She didn't want the evening to end, but all too soon the door to her cabin loomed in front of them.

Lance pulled her close for a lip-crushing kiss, then tilted her face to his. "I really did enjoy tonight. Sleep well. Dream of me."

There was no doubt of that.

31

Molly opened her eyes to complete and utter darkness. But she wasn't alone. Breathing drifted across the room. "Who's there?" She sat upright, pulling the sheet to her chin.

"Time to get up, Miss Nicholson." The light clicked on, stabbing her eyes. She blinked against its glare.

Morrison took the five steps he needed until he towered over Molly on her bunk. His expression told her he'd accept no arguments as he pointed a .357 Magnum in her face. "I want my money."

"I don't have it." Oh, Lord, he was going to shoot her while she lay in bed. Well, if she was going to die anyway, she wouldn't make it easy for him.

"Get up. I have a surprise for you."

Molly released her death grip on the sheet and tugged her over-sized tee shirt low enough to afford her some modesty, before swinging her feet to the floor. She glanced to the nightstand where her cell phone lay.

"Don't think about it." Morrison waved her toward the door. "We're going for a walk. Like two friends strolling the ship. Shout for help, and I'll shoot you and whoever is around. Maybe your boyfriend. How's that?"

Despite the perspiration trickling down her spine,

and the shaking in her limbs, Molly moved in front of him and out the door. *Lord, let Lance find me. Without getting himself killed.* No one roamed the halls. The hum of fluorescent lights sounded abnormally loud in the silence. She took a deep breath. "Which way?"

"Down. Through the engine room. We're going to a party."

"But I'm not dressed for a party."

He jabbed her in the back with the gun. "Funny girl. Start walking."

One of the cleaning staff approached. Morrison grabbed Molly and nuzzled her neck. "Smile, like you like it, or I'll waste him."

She swallowed back the bile and forced a smile to her face. The crewmember winked and continued past them. Once he turned the corner, Molly elbowed Morrison and slipped free of his grasp. "Get your hands off me!"

"Elbow me again, and I'll break your arm."

Molly quickened her pace, hoping to leave the man behind. When she started running, he grabbed her by the hair and yanked her back, and put his lips against her ear. "You are trying my patience!"

"I'll try to be more cooperative." Not really. All she needed was the slightest opportunity to get away, and she'd make a run for freedom.

They'd stopped in front of the elevator. Should she pray for it to be occupied? No. She didn't want to see a soul. Morrison would likely follow through on his threat. The doors pinged open.

Empty.

They stepped inside and she pressed the button for the lower level. When the car stopped, she led the way through the galley and opened a door marked engine room.

One of the cooks preparing breakfast gave her a questioning look. Morrison grinned and put a finger to his lips. The man acted like he zipped his lips closed and turned back to his job.

Molly frowned. Did people sneak off into remote corners of the ship often? Everyone acted like they were in on a fun secret. If not for Morrison's promise to shoot anyone who tried to help, Molly would've attracted attention when they spotted the first crew member.

They stepped into another hallway. A screw stuck out from a shelf and Molly brushed against it, leaving a piece of fabric, along with some skin, behind. Knowing Lance, he'd scour the entire ship to find her. She'd leave crumbs behind like Hansel and Gretel.

Natasha leaned against the door to the engine room, her arms crossed. A thump thump from the propeller blades echoed behind her. A loud hissing noise accompanied the mind numbing sound.

"Where's the money?" Natasha strode toward them.

Morrison lifted his weapon and fired one round between her eyes. "No need to share more than we have to. Miss Nicholson, please drag her into that closet."

Tears stung Molly's eyes. "Have you no value for human life?"

He shrugged. "Only when it suits me."

She grabbed Natasha's ankles and struggled to stuff the woman in a closet the size of a shower stall.

"Now grab some rags and cleaner and clean up this mess. We can't leave a trail."

Reaching past the body, Molly squelched the bile

rising in her esophagus and selected the needed supplies, then dropped to her knees. *Please, God. Get me out of this.* The tears she'd been holding back spilled over, mixing with the astringent cleanser and blood on the tiled floor. What was he waiting for? Why didn't he kill her now?

Her hands shook so much it was all she could do to hold the rag. Her throat ached from holding back sobs.

If Morrison held any weapon besides a gun, she'd tackle him and make a run for it. Instead, she had to suffer the humiliation and terror of waiting for the right chance. Or his decision to shoot her.

"That's enough." Morrison kicked her in the thigh. "Put everything away and let's get moving. He's waiting."

"Who?" Molly's hands shook so hard the cleanser fell from the shelf as soon as she set it into place. She kicked the bottle out of the way and slammed the door.

"You'll find out soon enough." He motioned for her to continue ahead of him.

They stepped into the engine room and headed to the back where a man turned to face them. "Cohn? But we saw you fall overboard." Molly's knees threatened to give way.

"A ploy and a clever use of quick release clasps." He rubbed his hands together. "Now, where's my money?"

That question quickly grew old. Molly squared her shoulders. "I don't have it."

Two steps put Cohn face-to-face with her. His backhanded slap sent her reeling into the wall. Her head banged against the drywall, bringing spots before her eyes.

"Stick her in there until she's ready to talk."

Morrison grabbed her by the arm, shoved her into a bent position, then crammed her into an empty cabinet. Her knees rested against her nose.

"Someone's coming. We'll question her again later. Maybe she'll be ready to tell us where our money is." The sound of stampeding feet rushed past her prison.

A sob ripped from Molly's throat as the lock engaged from the other side. She hated small, dark spaces.

A Bible verse from her childhood came to mind. Something about God's light. Why couldn't she remember?

The nurse at the hospital said God would never leave her nor forsake her. Did that include tiny, cramped spaces?

*

Lance knocked on Molly's door. When she didn't answer, he knocked again, then tried the knob. The door swung open easily at his touch. His heart plummeted. Withdrawing his weapon from the waistband of his pants, he stepped inside.

"Molly?"

The bed had been slept in. Her cell phone sat on the nightstand. Her camera bag rested under the bed. The open bathroom door showed him the room was empty.

Fear rushed through him with the speed of light. They'd taken her. Without anyone telling him, he knew. How'd they get in? He whirled and dashed to the security office.

Not bothering to knock, he barged in and planted both hands on Jack Morley's desk. His gun clattered against the top.

Morley's eyes widened and he straightened in his seat. "You can't have that here."

"I've a license to carry. Did you take Natasha's pass card when she switched cabins?"

"Of course. Why?"

"Molly Nicholson is gone."

"Gone where?"

Lance closed his eyes. "If I knew that, I wouldn't be here. I think she's been abducted. We need to search the ship." He speared Morley with a glance. "And if you dare say she jumped overboard like Hilga, I'll leap across this desk and throttle you."

Hilga! She would've had a pass card before going over. The question of how access was gained to Molly's room was answered. The question now, is who?

Morley shoved to his feet and waved to the two others in the office. "Get a move on. Scour the ship for Molly Nicholson. Keep walkie-talkies to channel two and let me know if you see anything out of the ordinary."

He tossed a radio to Lance, who caught it in one hand. "Thanks!" If he kidnapped someone, where would he take them? As far from passengers as possible. "I'm searching the lower deck."

Morley nodded. "Spread out everyone! Time is of the essence."

Lance dashed from the office and toward the stairs. Taking the elevator would bring him into contact with passengers. Something he wasn't in the mood for.

He stopped short on the first landing and dropped to his knees. "Lord, help me. Help me find her before it's too late. Keep her safe beneath your wings. Let her lie down like the wings of a dove covered with silver."

He needed to get control of himself. He'd be no good to Molly if he was a nervous wreck. Using the stair rail, he pulled himself to his feet and headed into the bowels of the ship.

Several crew members pushing carts piled with towels and bedding squeezed past him. Lance stopped in front of one of the women. "Excuse me. I'm looking for Molly Nicholson. Have you seen her?"

"No English." They shoved past him, eyeing his weapon.

Frustration weighed his heart as he watched them leave, and tucked the gun back into his waistband. Somebody had to have seen something. He'd question everyone onboard if he had to. He shoved open the double doors leading to the galley.

The kitchen resembled an ant hill with chefs and workers scurrying in every direction. Lance grabbed a metal ladle and a pan, then started banging. A woman shrieked, and what seemed like a multitude of faces turned to glare.

"I'm looking for a woman named Molly Nicholson." He lowered the utensil and pan. "She may have gone through here with a man or a woman. Has anyone seen her?"

They shook their heads. One man stepped forward. "But we aren't the night crew. Depending on who saw her would depend on the time."

Lance rubbed both hands over his face. *God, a sign, please. A blinking neon light. An idea. Anything.*

He lowered his arms. "Where's the most remote area of the ship?"

One of the galley workers jerked his thumb over his shoulder. "Engine room."

A metal door was tucked away in the corner. "Is there anyone there?"

"Off and on. When they need to check on things."

Lance headed that way. As he raised his hand to shove through, he spotted a piece of royal blue fabric hung on a nail. He plucked the scrap and held it up. "Any idea who this belongs to?"

More head shaking. Bingo! His sign. Bless you, Molly.

Lance barged through the door and dashed down the hall. As he rounded a corner, his legs slipped from beneath him. He flailed his arms like a windmill and fell flat on his back. The strong smell of bleach stung his nostrils.

32

Molly wrapped her arms around her legs, laid her cheek on her knees, and let the tears flow. Locked in a cabinet like a bucket of fish, the engine roaring and banging, no one would hear her yell unless they were standing on top of her.

The dark closed in, suffocating her, robbing her prison of oxygen. Her breath came fast, at hyperventilating speed. Molly grew dizzy. She couldn't pass out. Not now. What if someone came and she could cry for help? She took deep, slow breaths and willed her heart rate to return to normal.

How long until Cohn or Morrison came back to check on her? They said she'd only be in here until she came to her senses, right? Well, they could wait a long time. Frightened or not, she wouldn't give them the satisfaction of caving and telling them where the money was. Besides, then they'd most likely shoot the purser, and she couldn't live with that.

Weren't there guys who looked after the engines? Would they hear her cry for help, or had Cohn and Morrison shot them too? Her face burned from the trail her tears left.

God, are you here? Your Word says you'll never leave us alone. Do you stay, even if the plan is for us to die?

Not that she wanted to die. She wanted to experience a relationship with Lance. Succeed or not, she wanted the opportunity to try. Stuck in the inky blackness disrupted only by a sliver of amber light glowing around the cabinet hinges, she admitted she loved the bossy, sometimes overbearing,

Officer Lance Spencer.

Instead of bringing her joy, the realization brought on the tears in a deluge of emotion. She should've told him. She knew long before this day. The moment she realized how special he was—how different from Vince—she should've declared her feelings. Now, it might be too late.

Not only did she want a life with Lance, but one with God too. Heaven might be a wonderful place, but she wasn't ready to find out. Was a desire to live wrong, knowing what waited after death?

Was that a footstep? A scrape of someone passing? She screamed until she thought her throat would burst from the strain. No one came to free her. She closed her eyes and resigned herself to whatever God's plan for her might entail.

*

"Uh." Lance rolled to his side, off the weapon digging into his spine. That would leave a bruise. He pushed to his feet, biting off the groan rising in his throat. How long had he laid on the floor?

He searched the floor. Traces of the liquid he'd slipped on left a trail from where he'd fallen to a nearby closet. He yanked the door open.

Natasha's lifeless body fell into him, pushing him back. He stopped her forward progression, instead lowering her gently to the floor. He knew she was dead, yet he checked for a pulse anyway. No heartbeat.

Molly! He scanned the hall in both directions. Please, God, don't let him be too late. How long did he lay on the floor? Had he passed out?

He raised a hand to the back of his head. A lump rose beneath his fingers. No time to worry about his own injuries. Time ticked away with each breath he took. Think, Lance. You're a cop. Don't let personal feelings get in the way of professionalism.

Where are you Molly? Why hadn't someone located Natasha's body? Seen the wet floor?

Pressing the button on his radio, he informed Morley of his location.

"You're right beside the engine room. If she's down there, that's where she'll be. The ship docks in half an hour. We have to find her and whoever took her before then. If they get off the ship and disappear into the city, we'll have a hard time finding them. We're on our way. Wait for us."

"Right." Thirty minutes? Lance clicked off, and sprinted down the hall. He wouldn't wait for anyone. Not when he might be close.

The noise from the engine room ricocheted against his eardrums as he burst into the cavernous space. Two men in crew uniforms turned and held up their hands at the sight of him brandishing his gun.

"Molly Nicholson. Where is she?" He had to yell to be heard above the noise.

They shook their heads.

"Start looking." Lance ripped open cabinets. "If you find one that's locked, open it."

One of the men tapped him on the shoulder. "There's a locked one over there, but it's a padlock. Not one of ours."

Lance whipped out the radio. "Morley. Engine room. Bring a bolt cutter." He clicked off, squatted in front of the cabinet, and banged.

"Molly!" God, help him. "Molly!"

A faint knock ensued from the other side. Lance closed his eyes and leaned his forehead against the cool metal. "I'm here. We're going to get you out." *Thank you, God. Thank you.*

It seemed like an eternity before Morley and another security officer joined him. Lance held out his hand for the bolt cutter, then snapped the lock. When he opened the door, Molly fell into his arms.

She flung her arms around his neck. "You found me."

Lance plastered her to him and claimed her lips. "I wouldn't have stopped until I did." He lifted her into his arms. "Let's have the doctor check you out." He carried her past the two crew members who watched with open mouths.

"No, Lance." She pushed against him and peered into his face. "It was Morrison and Cohn. They're working together. Morrison shot Natasha."

"I found her." They stepped into the elevator, along with Morley. "Cohn faked falling overboard."

"Morrison came into my room and ordered me out. They locked me in the cabinet until I'd tell them where the money is." She laid her head on his shoulder. "I didn't. They would've killed me anyway."

His arms tightened around her. The realization of how close he'd come to losing her, tore through him.

"All I could think about," She raised her head. "Was that I never had the chance to tell you that I love you. I prayed for that opportunity. God gave it to me. I love you, Lance Spencer."

He blinked back tears and spoke through the lump in his throat. "I love you, Molly Nicholson."

"I hate to break up this love fest," Morley interrupted. "But we only have a few minutes to find Morrison and Cohn."

*

Lance loved her! God hadn't left her to die in the cabinet! With that knowledge, Molly knew they'd find Morrison and Cohn. They couldn't fail. Not now. She slipped from Lance's arms to stand on her feet.

The elevator pinged at the lobby floor. Molly stepped out into a throng of people and a mountain-sized pile of luggage. How long had she been locked up? "No, no, no! We've docked." She dashed through the doors and onto the deck with Lance and Morley on her heels.

Leaning over the railing, she scanned the throng of passengers disembarking. Taxis lined the curb. She ran her gaze over the cars and spotted Cohn and Morrison getting into a taxi. "There!" She pointed and rushed down the gangplank. "Call the FBI!"

"Molly, wait!" Lance grabbed her arm.

She yanked free. "We have to stop them." She continued her sprint and flung herself on the hood of the cab. No way had she gone through all that she had in the last week to let the men responsible for the murders go free.

The driver bolted from inside and yelled something at her in words she didn't understand. Morrison and Cohn slid from the back seat.

Cohn lifted his gun toward her.

Molly's gaze locked with his. She smiled and narrowed her eyes.

Two men in black suits tackled him to the ground. The gun skittered beneath the vehicle.

"That was the dumbest, but bravest, thing I've ever seen anyone do." Lance pulled Molly from the car. "Don't ever do something like that again. I almost had a heart attack."

"But they were getting away. And those two men ruined what could've been a dream vacation." She grinned. With the adrenaline wearing off, her legs trembled, and she leaned into Lance. She'd acted without thinking, and it felt wonderful. For the first time in her life, she'd done something without dotting all the i's and crossing the t's.

Lance wrapped his arms around her and leaned his chin on her head. "I've been thinking about that. It would be a good idea to come back here on our honeymoon, don't you think?"

"I can't agree more. She raised her face for his kiss.

The End

Continue Reading to read chapter 1 of book 5, *A Secret to Die for*

Dear reader:

Poor Molly and Lance. Their cruise didn't turn out anything like they'd thought. But, they survived and found love. A satisfying ending after all. Reviews are important to an author. If you enjoyed Exposure at Sea, please leave a review here.

Check out Cynthia's other books at www.cynthiahickey.com

Other Books in the Overcoming Evil Series

Mistaken Assassin
Captured Innocence
Mountain of Fear
A Secret to Die For

To answer that I have to describe what I think is my responsibility as a thriller writer:
To give my readers the most exciting roller coaster ride of a suspense story I can possibly think of.
- Jeffery Deaver

Chapter 1

Darcie Thayer's legs wobbled as fear choked her.

She didn't want to run anymore. Life didn't matter. What they'd do to her before they killed her scared Darcie the most. Once they had what Tony had hid, they'd have no further need of her.

She stared at the quaint town spread in a kaleidoscope-pattern a thousand feet below. She couldn't find a safe place. Not even a small town in the middle of Nowhere, Arkansas would provide the refuge she sought, not this place. But, she had run out of options.

Grasping the want ads with her right hand, she clutched the fence rail constructed to keep the Ozark Mountain tourists from plunging to their deaths. Despite her queasiness of heights, Darcie wished she were a bird that could soar at will.

The wind grabbed the paper and sent it twisting and twirling off to the valley below. Her cotton skirt whipped around her knees, and she swayed forward. She stumbled back, her heart in her throat.

Lightning shot across the sky like the tentacles of an octopus. The air crackled with electricity. Thunder crashed. Darcie lifted the long peasant-style skirt above her knees and sprinted for her '69 Chevy Impala. She hated the car. Detested it really, but she'd lost everything when Tony died. Money, home, security, car…and her unborn child. This monstrous boat was all she owned.

Her hand rubbed across her stomach as she envisioned the baby she'd carried. She stopped beside the car and lifted her face to heaven to let the rain wash away her guilt. The sky grumbled louder. She ducked and yanked the vehicle door open and scrambled inside.

Tony had promised her a new life. One filled with hope. With promise. Empty promises. One selfish act and her world lay shattered at her feet like a bashed mirror. The future didn't seem worth pursuing.

Her grandmother's voice emerged from the recesses of her mind. "Don't worry about tomorrow. Today has enough problems of its own." If so, then reliving the past was just as much a waste of time.

"Now what?" Darcie asked her reflection in the rearview mirror. "I've lost the address to my new job. All I know is the guy's name. York Wardell. An author who wants a live-in nanny to care for his kids. Probably while he writes the next great American novel." She scoffed and brushed wet bangs from her face. "Well, ready or not, here I come. Somebody around here is bound to know where the guy lives."

The drive down the mountain, with thunder booming around her, left Darcie's hands white-knuckled and shaking. She glanced at her watch and groaned. An hour late. She'd told the man she'd arrive for dinner. They'd agreed it would be a perfect time for her to get acquainted with the children. Would her new boss buy her excuse that she got lost?

She maneuvered her four-wheeled monstrosity into the first fast food drive-through she came to. Along with placing an order for a hamburger and fries, she asked the kid behind the window whether he knew of a York Wardell.

"Sure. He coaches the high school football team. At least until they get someone else hired." The pimply-faced youth pointed west and spouted off a list of directions as twisting as a country road.

"Thanks. I think I'll find it." Darcie peeled rubber out of the parking lot and headed in the direction of yet another mountain. "Great," she mumbled around a mouthful of ground beef. "It's getting dark, it's raining, and I've got to find this guy's house during a storm. Can life get any better?"

She'd almost made it to the top when her tire blew. Darcie stomped the brakes and sent the car into a skid. She dropped her hamburger.

Which way were you supposed to steer? Into the skid or away? Left? Right? She decided on left and jerked the wheel.

The Impala fishtailed on the wet blacktop. The steel divider between the road and emptiness loomed. Her stomach plunged like Niagra Falls. A scream ripped free of her throat.

The car skidded along the rail. Metal against metal screeched as piercing as a siren. She closed her eyes and prayed, even though she'd convinced herself God no longer cared.

The car finally shuddered to a stop. Darcie cut the ignition and slammed against the door. Locked. Pain radiated up her shoulder. After a few more lunges and grasping of slippery fingers on the lock, she got the door open and slid from the seat.

She slipped through the mud as she circled the car to check for damage. The passenger side sported a curved-in wide swatch of unpainted metal.

"And I thought you were ugly before." Darcie sniffed and leaned against the hood. "Now what do I do?"

She folded her arms across her chest, stared into the dark sky, and blinked against the falling drops. "Did you hear me, God? What do I do now? Could you maybe make it rain harder? How about some closer lightning? You know how much I love storms."

The sky lit in a brilliant display of fire. Darcie dove inside the car.

Rain pounded the roof, deafening in its ferocity. She wrapped her arms around her middle, hoping to find warmth. She sulked, shivered, and yelled. At God. When her watch showed ten o'clock, she grabbed her purse, suitcase, and keys, then exited into a drizzle.

Her feet slipped in her wet sandals. The sodden skirt tangled around her legs. Thighs trembling from the uphill climb, she stopped before collapsing in a soggy heap beside the road.

It's too soon. I'm not ready to begin life again. A year wasn't enough. I need five years. Ten years. The ever-present risk of danger hovered over her. How could she subject someone else's family to potential threat? Hiding on top of a mountain didn't guarantee they wouldn't find her. Especially since they'd come for her at the hospital. She shrugged. Finding what her husband had hid was top priority. She'd do whatever it took.

Darcie wrapped her arms around her knees and clenched

her chattering teeth. Where did she go from here? Farther up apparently, but the clouds covered the moon and stars. She sat in darkness.

The drizzle finally stopped. Sounds seemed magnified. Not being a country girl since she'd left home at eighteen, Darcie's heart beat an unnatural rhythm every time the woods around her popped, splashed, or snapped. *You've got to move, girl. If you don't, you'll be a bear's dinner*.

With that encouraging thought, she rose and continued. Blisters formed between her toes from the prong of the sandals. Her temper smoldered, and her rolling suitcase weighed five hundred pounds. She stumbled on a rock, stubbing her toe. Pain shot through her foot, and she gasped.

Headlight beams sliced through the night. Darcie squinted and raised a hand to shield her eyes.

The truck, an older model, passed. Water sprayed from its tires. drenching her further. Darcie gritted her teeth and turned to glare. She ought to do more than stare. Flee, in case the truck held her pursuers. But exhaustion hovered just under the surface.

Relief mingled with fear flooded her body as the vehicle turned back in her direction. Too tired to care, Darcie collapsed. Let them kill her.

The Ford stopped. Its beams dimmed. The driver-side door opened, and a cowboy boot-covered foot emerged to plant firmly on the ground. Darcie allowed her gaze to travel up the denim-clad legs as the man stepped in front of the lights. He towered above her. Her heart accelerated.

"Are you all right?" A rich baritone swept over her. The apparent knight in shining truck knelt before her.

Darcie glanced into dark eyes framed by wire-rimmed glasses. The eyes were set into the most handsome face she'd ever seen. A face so good-looking, it should only appear on the pages of a magazine. Her breath caught. She had to be hallucinating.

"Miss?"

She shook her head to clear it. "I've had an accident."

"You wouldn't be Darcie Thayer by any chance, would you?" He placed a hand beneath her elbow and helped her to her feet.

"York Wardell?" This couldn't be her boss. Luck didn't run that way for her. Or maybe it did. What a wonderful way to meet a new employer. Wet and bedraggled.

"The one and only. Where's your car?"

"About a mile back with a flat tire."

York led her to the passenger side of the pickup. "I'll take you to the house. We'll pick up your car tomorrow."

Darcie folded her arms and sank back into the seat. "I got lost. Then I got the flat tire and almost went sailing off the mountain. I apologize for being late."

"The kids have gone to bed. The housekeeper is watching them." He glanced at her. "You'll have to meet them tomorrow."

"It was really out of my control."

A muscle twitched in his jaw. "It's fine."

Okay, how fitting. A beautiful face with a nasty attitude. Her spirit sank. She wanted Tony back. Faults and all. At least they'd understood each other.

"The main thing is, you're okay." She looked like a drowned rat and, in spite of himself, York felt a tug on his heart as he stared at her. She looked too young to be a nanny. She'd said twenty-eight, but he swore she couldn't be older than nineteen. Red hair hung limp around a face with sparkling golden eyes and just a sprinkle of freckles across her nose.

When he'd driven past and noticed her slumped like a lump on the side of the road, he'd thought at first she was injured. After he discovered she'd only been stupid enough to walk in the dark, he'd felt the first stirrings of anger—at himself for feeling pity and for her—he shrugged. No reason to be mad at her. It was nothing but bad timing with a flat tire.

It didn't help that she was pretty, despite her drenching. After Michelle's betrayal, the last thing he needed, or wanted, was to entertain thoughts of another woman. He definitely didn't need a tiny slip of a woman complicating things. And York knew his weaknesses. The major one: a pretty face or a damsel in distress.

"How did you know where to find me?" Darcie swiped wet hair out of her face.

"There's only one road on and off this mountain unless you drive all the way around. It wasn't hard."

"Oh." Her hand cradled her stomach, almost protectively, as she glanced behind them.

"Are you hurt? Sick? Looking for someone?" York peered in the rearview mirror.

No, why?" Darcie straightened.

"Just wondering." She'd touched her stomach the way Michelle had when she was pregnant with Sam and Sarah. *Please don't let her be pregnant.* There isn't exactly a cornucopia of nannies in this part of the state. *And, forgive me, Lord, but he had a deadline to meet.*

York sighed. When had he gotten so mean? When Michelle died, that's when. With someone new living in the house, he vowed to work on his attitude.

They made the rest of the drive in silence. Occasionally, she'd shiver and wrap her arms tightly around her middle. York's gut clenched as sympathy for her increased. He ought to be more compassionate. Isn't that what the Bible taught? "I'm sorry I don't have a blanket or jacket, but we'll be home soon. Have you eaten?"

"Yes, thank you. I grabbed a burger when I stopped for directions. I'm sorry for the inconvenience. I really appreciate you coming to look for me." Darcie turned to face him. "I'll have breakfast ready by seven a.m., and the children dropped off at school by eight. If I can borrow a car, that is. Then what do I do?"

"Whatever you want. Cooking isn't part of your job description. I have a housekeeper. You'll be free until you pick the kids up at three. School is out in a week. You'll be plenty busy then."

"Great." She stared into the side mirror.

"Are you sure you aren't looking for someone?" Car lights pierced the night behind them.

"Positive. I'm just tired."

She sounded obstinate, her voice soft, yet hard as steel. York struggled to keep from smiling. He'd have difficulty taking such a small thing serious if she got really angry. Like a furious forest sprite. He'd known the woman five minutes, and she'd already shown she had two sides to her.

Two sides that traded places faster than a tornado could blow apart a trailer park. But, could she handle a couple of hurricanes named Sam and Sarah?

Scan this code to learn more

www.cynthiahickey.com

Cynthia Hickey is a multi-published and best-selling author of cozy mysteries and romantic suspense. She has taught writing at many conferences and small writing retreats. She and her husband run the publishing press, Winged Publications. They live in Arizona and Arkansas, becoming snowbirds with three dogs. They have ten grandchildren who keep them busy and tell everyone they know that "Nana is a writer."

Connect with me on FaceBook
Twitter
Sign up for my newsletter and receive a free short story
www.cynthiahickey.com

Follow me on Amazon
And Bookbub
Shop my bookstore here. For better price and autographed.

Enjoy other books by Cynthia Hickey

Misty Hollow
Secrets of Misty Hollow
Deceptive Peace
Calm Surface

Lightning Never Strikes Twice

Lethal Inheritance

Bitter Isolation

Say I Don't

Christmas Stalker

Stay in Misty Hollow for a while. Get the entire series here!

The Seven Deadly Sins series

Deadly Pride

Deadly Covet

Deadly Lust

Deadly Glutton

Deadly Envy

Deadly Sloth

Deadly Anger

The Tail Waggin' Mysteries

Cat-Eyed Witness

The Dog Who Found a Body

Troublesome Twosome

Four-Legged Suspect

Unwanted Christmas Guest

Wedding Day Cat Burglar

Brothers Steele

Sharp as Steele

Carved in Steele

Forged in Steele

Brothers Steele (All three in one)

The Brothers of Copper Pass
Wyatt's Warrant
Dirk's Defense
Stetson's Secret
Houston's Hope
Dallas's Dare
Seth's Sacrifice
Malcolm's Misunderstanding
The Brothers of Copper Pass Boxed Set

Time Travel
The Portal

Tiny House Mysteries
No Small Caper
Caper Goes Missing
Caper Finds a Clue
Caper's Dark Adventure
A Strange Game for Caper
Caper Steals Christmas
Caper Finds a Treasure
Tiny House Mysteries boxed set

Wife for Hire – Private Investigators
Saving Sarah
Lesson for Lacey
Mission for Meghan

CYNTHIA HICKEY

Long Way for Lainie
Aimed at Amy
Wife for Hire (all five in one)

A Hollywood Murder
Killer Pose, book 1
Killer Snapshot, book 2
Shoot to Kill, book 3
Kodak Kill Shot, book 4
To Snap a Killer
Hollywood Murder Mysteries

Shady Acres Mysteries
Beware the Orchids, book 1
Path to Nowhere
Poison Foliage
Poinsettia Madness
Deadly Greenhouse Gases
Vine Entrapment
Shady Acres Boxed Set

CLEAN BUT GRITTY Romantic Suspense

Highland Springs

Murder Live
Say Bye to Mommy
To Breathe Again
Highland Springs Murders (all 3 in one)

Colors of Evil Series

Shades of Crimson
Coral Shadows

The Pretty Must Die Series

Ripped in Red, book 1
Pierced in Pink, book 2
Wounded in White, book 3
Worthy, The Complete Story

Lisa Paxton Mystery Series

Eenie Meenie Miny Mo
Jack Be Nimble
Hickory Dickory Dock
Boxed Set

Hearts of Courage
A Heart of Valor
The Game
Suspicious Minds
After the Storm
Local Betrayal
Hearts of Courage Boxed Set

Overcoming Evil series
Mistaken Assassin
Captured Innocence

Mountain of Fear

Exposure at Sea

A Secret to Die for

Collision Course

Romantic Suspense of 5 books in 1

INSPIRATIONAL

Nosy Neighbor Series

Anything For A Mystery, Book 1

A Killer Plot, Book 2

Skin Care Can Be Murder, Book 3

Death By Baking, Book 4

Jogging Is Bad For Your Health, Book 5

Poison Bubbles, Book 6

A Good Party Can Kill You, Book 7

Nosy Neighbor collection

Christmas with Stormi Nelson

The Summer Meadows Series

Fudge-Laced Felonies, Book 1

Candy-Coated Secrets, Book 2

Chocolate-Covered Crime, Book 3

Maui Macadamia Madness, Book 4

All four novels in one collection

The River Valley Mystery Series

Deadly Neighbors, Book 1

EXPOSURE AT SEA

The Red Hat's Club (Contemporary novellas)

Short Story